The Toplofty Lord Thorpe

The Toplofty Lord Thorpe

KASEY MICHAELS

THORNDIKE
CHIVERS

This Large Print edition is published by Thorndike Press®, Waterville, Maine USA and by BBC Audiobooks, Ltd, Bath, England.

Published in 2004 in the U.S. by arrangement with Harlequin Books S.A.

Published in 2004 in the U.K. by arrangement with Harlequin Enterprises II BV.

U.S. Hardcover 0-7862-5911-6 (Famous Authors)
U.K. Hardcover 0-7540-9949-0 (Chivers Large Print)
U.K. Softcover 0-7540-9860-5 (Camden Large Print)

The text of this Large Print edition is unabridged.
Other aspects of the book may vary from the original edition.

Set in 16 pt. Plantin by Minnie B. Raven.

Printed in the United States on permanent paper.

British Library Cataloguing-in-Publication Data available

Library of Congress Cataloging-in-Publication Data

Michaels, Kasey.
    The toplofty Lord Thorpe / Kasey Michaels.
      p. cm.
    ISBN 0-7862-5911-6 (lg. print : hc : alk. paper)
    1. Large type books.   I. Title.
  PS3563.I2725T67 2004
    813'.54—dc22   2003060050

For Maryanne Colas,
who has been there for the laughter . . .
and the tears.

PROLOGUE

My dearest Jennie, and Kit too, of course, It seems an age since last we saw each other, and had a long, comfortable coze, which of course it is not, considering that I stood as godmother to your darling Christopher not two months past. I am back in London now as you can see from the postmark, although Papa is not with me (as usual) and Aunt Rachel has been once more set to bear-lead me (again, as usual).

You know, dearest Jennie, that this will be my fourth Season since I first made my curtsy at St. James's. Papa says any chit with a whit of sense would have long since given it up and donned her caps, but he has agreed to finance one more foray, hoping against hope I shall at least catch myself a rich cit; but as I told Papa, what with Lady Cynthia's mama passing away so shortly into the Season last year, and with Lord Thorpe having so inconveniently retired to his estates as soon as was decent after the funeral, *my* latest

Hunting Season was rendered unusually short.

Lady C. is at last out of black gloves (so far this marriage of hers has been delayed by no less than three expiring relatives), and she and Lord Thorpe are once more in town, with the wedding date again set. I know you both believe me to be some sort of Don Quixote, forever tilting at windmills, but I do believe it is Fate, not Lady Cynthia's wilting relatives, that have delayed the nuptials until such time as I can convince Lord Thorpe he would be making a Dreadful Mistake.

I am the better woman for him, I know I am, so you — and especially you, Kit — may draw comfort from the knowledge that my intentions, if not my actions, are only of the purest. Lady Cynthia may bleed undiluted blue when she is pinked, but she is not only rude beyond conceiving, but a dead bore into the bargain. Julian — that is to say, Lord Thorpe — must be Saved from Her at All Costs. Of course, my loves, the fact that I am Absolutely Mad for the man barely enters into this At All.

But now that the couple in question is back in town, with poor Lord Thorpe lugging that sad, bland creature hither and thither, my opportunities shall again present themselves. Oh, Lord Thorpe may have already been situated in the city for a fortnight or so before his fiancée returned, but he spent his time at his various clubs, barely coming into society. It is strange, is it not, how men seem to enjoy such places, especially since one of my young gentlemen friends (nobody you'd know, Kit, as he didn't serve in the army) told me that the atmosphere in all these clubs is so dreadfully fusty — rather like being in some duke's residence, with the duke lying dead in his chambers upstairs.

Please forgive me if I ramble on — Aunt Rachel says it is my only forte — but you can see, can't you, how this is my last chance to make Julian aware of me? It is time I took the bull by the horns, as it were, for after all, I cannot continue to rely on Lady C.'s relatives to so obligingly keep cocking up their toes before each scheduled wedding date, now can I?

Kiss little Christopher hello — he is such a darling — and cross your fingers for me, just for luck you understand, for I am sure that this time I Cannot Fail to make Julian love me.

> Your most affectionate cousin,
> Lucy

Kit Wilde, Earl of Bourne, put down the missive after reading it aloud to his wife as she cradled their sleeping son. "She cannot fail, she says," he repeated, shaking his head rather sadly. "I can only wonder at her optimism, kitten, seeing as how the poor girl has made such a sad hash of things so far."

"Oh, I don't know, Kit," Jennie replied, absently stroking her son's soft blond curls. "You'd be surprised to know to what lengths a woman might be willing to travel in the name of love. For what it's worth," she proclaimed, grinning saucily at her doubting husband, "*my* blunt's on Cousin Lucy!"

CHAPTER ONE

It was a truly lovely early-spring day, unseasonably fair and fine, especially when one considered the depressingly lengthy stretch of damp and drizzle that had so far this month curtailed outings in the park for all but the most dedicated or desperate promenaders, the former intent on exercising their horseflesh and the latter committed to the pursuit of elusive eligible bachelors, bits of juicy gossip, and cards of invitation to the most select social gatherings on offer.

Quite naturally this bright, sunshiny day found anybody and everybody converging on the park with a vengeance; the resultant crush of curricles, high-perch phaetons, ancient landaus, barouches, skittish, prancing saddle horses, and hopeful pedestrians quickly spilling over from the gravel paths to cut deep ruts into the soft turf and carelessly trample down the shrubberies.

Julian Rutherford, Earl of Thorpe, and his fiancée of long standing, Lady Cynthia Buxley, had been in the park upwards of an hour, having arrived with the notion that a lively canter for the length of the park and back atop their overly fresh mounts would make an enjoyable change from the inactivity the weather had enforced upon them.

To their combined chagrin, however, the only exertion either had thus far expended was by way of a constant tug-of-war with their high-spirited horses, who demonstrated their disappointment at the snail's pace necessarily set by their masters by alternately snorting, prancing, and tossing their heads in their eagerness to be off.

"This is perfectly beastly, Julian," Lady Cynthia complained in dreadful accents for perhaps the hundredth time. "How I abhor Sundays in the park, what with every upstart cit and ragged peasant given free access just as if they had a right to be here. I tell you, Julian, if we are not careful we will suffer the same dread fate as our fellow aristocrats in France. Stop it, Egyptian Dawn," she commanded firmly, breaking off her complaining to bring her mount back under control.

"Go easy on her mouth, Cynthia," Lord Thorpe cautioned as the woman hauled down sharply on the reins. "We'll be nearing a gate shortly, upon which time I suggest we disengage ourselves from this ridiculous parade and I escort you home. If it weren't for the multitude of acquaintances demanding our attention, holding our progress to an infuriating crawl, we should have been gone long since. It is only our popularity you have to blame, my dear, for our virtual imprisonment within this crush of humanity. Your friends have been too long without you, and feel the need of a few moments to renew their friendship."

"And to reiterate their sympathy concerning my sad loss," Lady Cynthia added, smoothing down the skirt of her dove-gray riding dress. "I do hope no one thought me fast to have come out of my blacks so soon after Mama's passing."

"A year is quite proper, Cynthia," her fiancé assured her matter-of-factly, neglecting to add that she looked most becoming in her half-mourning, just as he had neglected to show so much as a moment's concern over the possibility of Egyptian Dawn bolting in her agitation, and the resultant threat to life and limb this would present to his beloved.

They progressed along the path slowly but steadily, deigning only to bow or wave to the many who would have them stop beside their conveyances for a chat, and were almost to the gate when Egyptian Dawn, momentarily given her head as Lady Cynthia called a greeting to a turbaned dowager frantically trying to gain her attention, rolled her eyes wildly and reared, nearly unseating her rider.

Thorpe reacted quickly, grabbing for the mare's halter before the horse could gather her legs back under her and break into a dangerous gallop, and while nearby spectators alternately shrieked and swooned, he expertly brought Egyptian Dawn back under control.

"Whatever happened to spook her so?" Lady Cynthia asked, looking around her to see that Egyptian Dawn was not the only horse so disturbed. All around them tigers were running to calm their masters' frightened teams, while pedestrians prudently sprinted from out of the way of slashing hooves.

And then Lord Thorpe caught a movement off to his left and swung around in the saddle to get a better look at the flash of ruby red that was speeding down a nearby slope, heading directly for them. His light gray eyes narrowed as he sought to identify what looked to be some female person who was, unbelievably, perched precariously between a larger pair of rap-

14

idly advancing narrow-spoked wheels. "What the devil?" he was startled into saying, reaching wildly for his quizzing glass.

Attracted by her companion's rare descent into exclamation, Lady Cynthia looked at him askance, and then followed his lead and cast her gaze onto the nearby slope. "Oh, no," she muttered in an extremely unladylike style. "It is that dratted Gladwin girl again. Whatever can she be about this time?"

By now all in the vicinity had spied out the cause of their animals' unrest and a minor uproar was in progress, with lords and ladies shaken from their usual sangfroid into garbled speech and a few members of the lower orders, in the park on their off day, cheering and yelling and generally encouraging the rider of what looked to be one of "dem newfangled hobbyhorses, like," to "give 'er all she's got, girlie!"

The rider, so cheered by her encouraging audience, lifted one gloved hand from the wooden cross-balance board to acknowledge them with a wave, a maneuver that nearly brought her to grief when the front wheel struck a small rock and for a short time her vehicle listed dangerously to one side. But that she was no novice to this mode of transportation was soon to be seen, for she made short work of leaning her forearm more heavily on the far side of the cross-balance board and redirecting the hobbyhorse onto more level ground.

As she dragged her jean-covered toes in the soft grass alongside the path, however, she soon realized that the advertisement lauding the hobbyhorse as being designed to allow her "drapery to flow loosely and elegantly to the ground" to be sadly inaccurate, as she felt the spring breeze ballooning her skirts and cooling her, at the moment, indecently exposed ankles, to the delight of all and sundry.

"It *is* Lucy Gladwin, Julian, just as I said," Lady Cynthia informed her companion unnecessarily, as anyone with two eyes in his head could not help but recognize that flamboyant young lady who had been setting the *ton* on its collective head for the past three Seasons. And, as if her face and figure were not sufficiently familiar, the young hussar standing nearby had confirmed the fact just moments before by shouting, "It's Old Hale and Hearty's girl, Lucy. What a great gun! Pluck to the backbone!"

"Old Hale and Heart indeed," the earl spat contemptuously. "Sir Hale Gladwin has much to answer for in his outrageous daughter. You'd think he'd marry her off to some backwater squire who'd keep her from making a fool of herself in town."

"Indeed yes," his fiancée agreed, preening her hair complacently, secure in the knowledge that *she*, the daughter of an earl and cognizant of both the responsibility and privilege of rank, would never allow herself to become such a spectacle. "Sir Hale, who is ramshackle past reclaim himself, probably due to some sad underbreeding of his ancestors, should be made to contain his daughter's mad starts or else remove her from polite society altogether. Such a vulgar, shameless creature."

The vulgar, shameless creature, she of the unattending father, had at last dragged her vehicle to a stop just where she had planned — directly in front of the Earl of Thorpe. "Good day to you, my lord," she chirped merrily as, unthinking of her windblown appearance, she gave him the full benefit of her dazzling smile.

Lord Thorpe, from his vantage point high above her, looked at her through his quizzing glass, intent on wiping that inane grin from her face. Lucy, small and dark-

17

haired, was in full looks when dressed in red, and her sparkling eyes, ruby lips, and flushed cheeks gave her an all-over look of fresh, untrammeled beauty that caused the earl to shudder. It wasn't decent, nor was it fitting, for a female to look quite so . . . so abandoned. It was enough to stir a man's blood in a highly uncomfortable way, as he silently acknowledged by shifting slightly in the saddle.

"Miss Gladwin," he said now, condescending to favor her with a slight, very slight, bow. "I would deem it a kindness if you were to remove your, er, machine from the immediate vicinity. Its presence has greatly agitated Lady Cynthia's mount, and your continued presence brings the possibility of injury to both of you."

"What? My hobbyhorse?" Lucy questioned, shaking her head. "What a silly animal to be frightened by such a thing. Why, in my opinion a hobbyhorse is —"

"I do not remember requesting your opinion, Miss Gladwin," Lord Thorpe cut in sharply, finally succeeding in wiping the smile from that young female's face. "I cannot, in fact, remember ever requiring anything from you other than your absence. Do I make myself clear, Miss Gladwin?"

As far as set-downs go, this one was definitely first-rate, and Lucy, sadly crushed by his harsh words, was foolish enough to lift her face to Lady Cynthia in mute appeal. If she had hoped for any tenderness from that quarter, however, she had sadly mistaken her woman. Looking down her rather long, aristocratic nose, Lady Cynthia added repressively, "Indeed, Miss Gladwin. Not only have you yet again made a complete fool of yourself, but you have become, at least to us, more than a little boring. For three Seasons now you have been dogging our every step, so it seems, until I vow myself to be quite out of patience with you. It would be a kindness, to us as well as to yourself, if you would simply *go away*."

For one brief moment Lucy's dimpled chin betrayed a lamentable tendency to quiver, bringing forth an involuntary flutter of sympathy from the earl while prompting the production of a most self-satisfied smirk upon Lady Cynthia's thin face. While Lucy may have briefly entertained the thought of playing on Lord Thorpe's tender feelings (feelings which, there were legions who would willingly swear, did not exist), the sight of her rival's smug expression kept her from summoning up a tear in favor of taking that infuriating female down a peg or two.

"Why, Lady Cynthia, whatever do you mean?" Lucy asked innocently, assuming an air of genuine anxiety. "Do you often have this feeling of being followed? My Great-Uncle Herbert was just so afflicted, you know." She turned to look up at Lord Thorpe, who was rapidly adjusting his opinion of Miss Gladwin as being a brainless widgeon in need of rescue. "In Great-Uncle Herbert's case it was much the same; always telling us how people were staring at him, plotting against him." She shook her head. "They had to put him in Ringmoor, poor man. Nasty business it was, too, what with the chains and all."

"Oh! You *horrid* creature!" Lady Cynthia exclaimed shrilly, momentarily abandoning her role of earl's daughter for that of a highly indignant female. "Julian! She has insulted me. *Do something!*"

"What do you suggest, my dear?" Lord Thorpe replied in his usual unemotional tone. "Pistols at dawn?"

Lady Cynthia was saved from further indiscretion (and Lord Thorpe from having to remind his betrothed that she was in danger of making a cake of herself in front of half the *ton*) by the arrival of Lucy's

Aunt Rachel, the older woman alighting from an open carriage that had just then pulled up alongside them.

"Here you are, Lucy," that harassed-looking lady said without preamble. "You promised to stay beside the carriage, dear. It took us forever to work our way around once you took off over that rise. Come away now, Lucy. It's time for tea."

"You are Miss Gladwin's keep . . . um . . . that is to say, are you in charge of this young lady?" Lord Thorpe asked, causing Aunt Rachel's thin shoulders to rise up protectively around her ears. If she had hoped, once she was close enough to see that her charge had once again landed in the brambles, that they just might be able to escape the scene with their skins intact, Lord Thorpe's deliberately rude question put a firm period to her hopes. Swallowing down hard on the lump of apprehension that had risen in her throat, the lady could do no more than turn and face her questioner, replying, "I am Rachel Gladwin, my lord, Miss Gladwin's aunt."

"You have my sympathy, Mrs. Gladwin," he responded, favoring her with a slight bow as he looked down at her from his lofty height.

"*Miss* Gladwin, my lord," Aunt Rachel

corrected. "I am Sir Hale's younger sister."

"Then I repeat my condolences twofold, ma'am, and hope you forgive me for requiring you to own up to the blood relationship in public. Therefore, since I feel it incumbent upon us to discuss what I believe to be a common problem, I will call upon you at your residence in the morning. Good day to you, ma'am," he concluded in a tone that made it clear he had dismissed her.

"And good day to you too, my lord," Lucy called after the two riders who had already begun edging their mounts on down the path, just as if she didn't know that they had cut her deliberately.

"Have Walter lift that horrid machine up behind the carriage, Lucy, and join me inside," her aunt instructed, already turning to be handed up onto the squabs. "We must hurry home so that I might indulge in a fit of the vapors. I do believe I have earned it."

"Oh, pooh, Aunt Rachel —" Lucy twinkled irrepressibly "— you never would be so missish."

"Knowing that your insufferable Lord Thorpe is coming to Portman Square tomorrow to ring a peal over my head about my delinquent niece may just be the nudge I needed to cultivate a tendency to find solace in nervous spasms. Oh yes," that lady went on imperturbably as her niece began to protest that Lord Thorpe was not about to do any such thing. "Or did you think he was coming to tell me he has fallen madly in love with you and has jilted Lady Cynthia so that the two of you can live happily ever after?"

Lucy squirmed comfortably against the squabs, a satisfied smile lighting her eyes. "The thought had occurred to me, my dear aunt. The thought had occurred."

CHAPTER TWO

Lucy awoke the following morning with a feeling of warm anticipation that was totally unmixed with any touches of anxiety. Lord Thorpe was coming to Portman Square in a few short hours. Lord Thorpe, the man she had first clapped eyes on over three years ago, instantly losing her heart to the tall blond gentleman who had, by his magnificent physical appearance, filled every one of her girlish requirements for a perfect mate.

The fact that this gentleman had not been similarly emotionally poleaxed by the mere sight of a young dark-haired miss in virginal white muslin did not serve to lessen her enthusiasm a whit. Neither did the information that the gentleman of her dreams was already engaged to be married.

Against the pleadings of her aunt, who told her to give up her childish fantasies and concentrate on hooking herself a more landable fish, Lucy set out to ensnare the earl with her feminine charms. Alas, he seemed immune to discreet flirting overtop her fan or coy eyelash batting directed at him from across the room.

Deciding that stronger measures were in order, she had then taken steps to call herself to his lordship's notice. As those steps involved, for the most part, impetuous mad starts, harmless escapades, and one or two nearly risque exploits, it was not too much longer before Lord Thorpe (not to mention the rest of fashionable London) was aware of Lucy Gladwin.

Society, always on the lookout for titillation, welcomed Lucy with open arms, and she was soon surrounded by a group of the more lively members of the *ton*, who thought her to be "a great gun."

Lord Thorpe, however, was not similarly impressed. Too late, Lucy discovered that her beloved was more than a little bit high in the instep and looked down upon people who, in his way of thinking, disgraced their lineage by their common behavior.

Anyone would be excused for believing that Lucy, once she discovered the arrogance that lay behind her intended's handsome face, would have washed her hands of the man and set out to discover a more suitable gentleman who would appreciate a woman like herself. But those foolish enough to consider such a possibility would likewise have been wise to refrain from laying odds on their supposition, for anyone choosing to put down his blunt on such an eventuality would soon be the poorer for his optimism, as Lucy was made of sterner stuff.

Positive she could not have been mistaken in her judgment of Lord Thorpe, Lucy had, over the years, got it into her head that the man was merely a victim of his birth and upbringing. There was a good, sweet, caring man beneath that pompous, straitlaced exterior, and she wasn't going to rest until the world at large (and Lord Thorpe in particular) was forced to acknowledge that fact.

For over three years Lord Thorpe, armed with his indifferences, had avoided publicly owning to his awareness of Lucy's none-too-subtle pursuit of his person. With his fiancée on his arm, he had chosen to pretend Lucy Gladwin did not really exist. His strategy had worked very well. Onlookers who at first snickered at Lucy's antics were quickly silenced by Lord Thorpe's chilling looks and sarcastic put-downs, and soon Lucy was regarded as nothing more than a darling, rather madcap eccentric, and Lord Thorpe's name was no longer linked with hers.

But her antics of the day before, warning him of yet another Season to be spent warding off her ridiculous bids for attention and overlooking her preposterous follies, had forced him to take action. Not for a moment (well, maybe for just a sublime second or two in time) did Lucy believe the earl was calling in Portman Square for any reason but to warn her off in that blood-chilling tone he employed to such advantage.

Lucy, just now snuggling back down under her covers, an inane smile on her face, would not have been blamed for being frightened out of her wits at the prospect of Lord Thorpe's bound-to-be-scathing diatribe. Indeed, most *men*, if faced with the fact that Lord Thorpe would be arriving at their domicile to verbally tear a strip off their hides, would have suddenly found pressing business in far-off Cumbria that required their immediate attention.

But Lucy was not dreading the confrontation one little bit. As a matter of fact, now that she had decided on a course of action, she was looking forward to the meeting with every indication of eagerness.

As Lord Thorpe tooled his matched grays through the early-morning traffic in

Mayfair, he rehearsed the speech he would soon be delivering to Miss Rachel Gladwin. Mentally adding a word here or erasing a too-severe phrase there, he wished yet again that Sir Hale Gladwin was in residence in Portman Square. After all, this was a conversation best handled between gentlemen — not that Sir Hale, that red-faced, hard-drinking, blustering fool, could be counted on to realize the gravity of the situation.

Sir Hale embraced a mode of behavior that was the complete antithesis of every value Julian Rutherford felt a gentleman should display. There were times, thought his lordship as he edged his curricle past a delivery wagon that had no business still being about at this hour, that he wished that wealth and good lineage were not the sole prerequisites for admission to polite society. There should be some kind of test, he mused reflectively, some sort of examination, as it were, for young peers, that would exclude all but the more intelligent, the better mannered, from their ranks.

That he, Lord Thorpe, would score at or near the top in such a test was a foregone conclusion. He was intelligent, erudite, possessed only the highest instincts, was worthy of the loftiest regard, and, in general, exemplified all that was desired in an English nobleman. Anyone who didn't believe it could apply to his mother — who had devoted her life to making her son aware of his perfection — and she would be happy to supply a full listing of his attributes.

That he was in addition — alas, also thanks to his proud mama — arrogant, autocratic, pompous, blindly biased in his opinions, and insufferably straitlaced never occurred to him (and who, pray tell was there brave enough or foolhardy enough to bring such failings to his attention?).

Once fully grown, and already self-satisfied to the point of smugness, Lord Thorpe had advanced to the age of three-and-thirty years, still warmed by the knowledge that his fellowmen had yet to do anything to undermine his fine opinion of himself — or his bad opinion of them.

So why had he, a man who held himself above the plebeian antics of the underbred, allowed this silly Gladwin chit to get so annoyingly under his skin — and worse yet, remain there for over three long, uncomfortable years? Surely he should have been able to continue his pretense of ignoring both her and her atrocious behavior? But that was just it — his indifference *was* a pretense. He had never really succeeded in banishing her from his conscious mind.

Not that he was intrigued by her vibrant, volatile personality, or attracted to her petite but still somewhat earthy charms. On the contrary, he was repelled by them, and angry at himself for allowing any hint of base physical attraction to the chit to disturb the even tenor of his days.

Physical desire was for the lower orders and young peers out on a romp. It was *not* for distinguished scions of ancient houses. Every time he was forced to acknowledge Lucy Gladwin's existence, it was like being served a slap in the face, a disturbing reminder that he was, after all, only human, and therefore susceptible to common carnal lust.

Well, he reminded himself as he thought fleetingly of the way Lucy had looked the day before in the park, there is no place in *my* life for such animal weakness. A gentleman does not desire women of his own social level in that way — such base cravings were reserved for liaisons with opera dancers and other low women, whose lesser intellect and poor breeding opened them to all sorts of licentious behavior. Imagine Cynthia abandoning her cool air of self-possession beneath him as they writhed about in bed — preposterous! He would lose all respect for her — the woman whom he had chosen to bear the next proud generation of Rutherfords.

Lady Cynthia. She was another reason behind this morning's visit to Portman Square. It was his duty to protect her from further upset. The earl had studied long and hard before condescending to offer his hand to this exemplary female — she of the impressive lineage, elevated social standing, high standards, and impeccable manners (and straight white teeth, for such things must be considered). Cynthia knew full well the responsibility placed upon her by her rank, and was comfortingly cognizant of both the honor and the duties that came along with his proposal of marriage.

That all her fine blue blood and careful upbringing did not keep her from bellowing at him like some common Billingsgate fishwife once they were clear of the park the day before, Lord Thorpe chose to charge to a justifiable bout of nerves caused by Lucy Gladwin's sad exhibition of hoydenism — although deep down he believed that Lucy's supposedly artless, wide-eyed set-down hinting of an imbalance in Lady Cynthia's mind had more than a little bit to do with the matter.

Raving that Miss Gladwin was, in her words, "an insupportable person," Cynthia had gone on at length about the trials she had endured thanks to that "silly chit dogging our every step and throwing herself at your head every chance she gets." That this tirade did not serve to turn his lordship's head, seeing as how he could not help but assume that he was both the target of Miss Gladwin's slavish adoration and the man who had inspired Lady Cynthia's unseemly display of jealousy, was only due to the fact that he already had a very high opinion of himself and saw nothing unusual in either of the ladies' reactions.

He had, by the time they had reached Lady Cynthia's residence in Grosvenor Square, succeeded in convincing his betrothed that all would be settled before another day was out, finally penetrating her near-hysteria over the thought of her fiancé actually volunteering to place himself under the same roof as that vulgar girl. "I seriously doubt I will even be forced to so much as lay eyes on Miss Gladwin, my dear," he had told her as the acrid smell of the burnt feathers Lady Cynthia's maid had lately been waving beneath her mistress' nostrils found him seeking recourse to his scented handkerchief. "I am tempted to believe the aunt is reasonably intelligent. Surely a few words meant to point her in the right direction will be all that is needed to put an end to this infantile charade once and for all. I'm only sorry I didn't act sooner."

Now, turning his pair into Portman Square, the earl was still of the same mind as when he gave his assurances to Lady Cynthia. He should have done this years ago and saved himself a great deal of trouble. So thinking, he threw the reins to his tiger as that slim young fellow ran to the horses' heads, and leapt lightly onto the flagway, determined to complete his interview with the elder Miss Gladwin in time to keep an appointment with his tailor before noon.

The earl was just in the process of spreading his coattails in preparation of seating himself in the bright, sunlit drawing room (choosing a wide, straight-backed armchair that he felt would cast him more in the role of host than guest, thereby gaining yet another subtle advantage on the sure-to-be-apprehensive Miss Rachel Gladwin) when a flurry of movement near the open double doors brought him back to a standing position.

The woman who had entered the room had her back to him for the moment, as she was fully occupied in bustling the reluctant butler away from the doorway. Once the elderly servant, just then whispering fiercely under his breath, was repositioned in the hallway so close to the entrance that his straining body looked as if it was imprisoned behind an invisible barrier of glass, the doors were firmly shut in his face — with or without inflicting a nasty pinch to the man's rather prominent proboscis, the earl was not to know.

"Now, then, my lord," Lucy Gladwin began, wiping her hands together as if in anticipation, "shall we get to it? To what do we owe the pleasure of your company?"

Lord Thorpe didn't answer at once, as he was caught between a silent inventory of Lucy's person, becomingly if not correctly (as it still lacked an hour till noon) attired in a formal gown of deep rose silk, and the dawning realization that the two of them were, most improperly too, alone together in a room whose doors he had just heard lock shut.

The twinkle he saw in Lucy's bright eyes was all the warning he needed (even if he were dense enough to overlook the distraught butler, the low-cut gown, and the bolted doors) to alert him to the fact that he had to do a good bit more than select the proper seat if he was going to convince Lucy — or himself — that *he* was in control of this interview.

Drawing himself up to his full, not unimposing height, he said coolly, "Tell me, Miss Gladwin, when you say 'we,' are you employing the kingly 'we' — or has your aunt mastered the art of invisibility?"

Lucy laughed and waved one small hand at him as if to say his little joke was amusing but not really worthy of a reply. Moving gracefully across the carpeting to stand in front of the settee, she inclined her head and bade her guest sit down and make himself comfortable.

"I shan't be staying," the earl informed her, already striding regally toward the door. "It isn't proper for you to receive male visitors without your chaperon present."

"Oh, pooh!" Lucy exclaimed airily, plunking herself down on the settee. "After all, who's to know if we don't tell?"

Thorpe pivoted neatly on his heels to face her and returned stonily, "*I* shall know, Miss Gladwin."

A wide smile rearranged Lucy's upturned face into a startling resemblance to the enchanting pixie princess featured in a favored storybook the earl had read during his days in the nursery and believed long since forgotten. "And will you *tell,* my lord?" she teased. "I didn't think earls tattled."

"That's enough, Miss Gladwin!" Thorpe decreed repressively, his palm itching to administer a few satisfying smacks to the chit's upturned derriere. "I bid you good day."

"No, you don't," Lucy answered serenely, arranging her skirts more becomingly as she eased back against the cushions of the green-and-white striped satin settee. "The doors are locked and *I've* got the key right here."

The earl, who was just about to grasp one of the door handles, turned his head just in time to see Lucy patting the neckline of her gown just at her bosom. Leaning his back against the door, he folded his arms and negligently crossed one foot in front of the other. "I always contended you were nothing more than a mischievous child. Now I see I was correct. What did you do with your aunt, you pernicious brat, lock her in the linen cupboard?"

Lucy had the good grace to blush. "Aunt

Rachel has been called to her good friend's bedside in Half Moon Street on a mission of mercy. It seems poor Mrs. Halstead has taken a nasty fall and broken her leg."

"Now, why do I doubt that? Or did you attack that poor lady just to avoid telling an untruth after all your other crimes?" the earl questioned suavely.

Tilting her head to one side, Lucy brazened it out, although she was not best pleased at the way things were going. Nothing was happening as she had thought it would when first she had hatched this scheme. "No, it is all a hum, a great bag of moonshine I invented to draw Aunt Rachel away at the crucial moment. I sent the note myself," she ended quite unnecessarily.

Her little face suddenly quite solemn, she sat upright and held her hands tightly clasped in her lap. "It was wicked of me, I know, but I had to see you — I just had to!"

His lordship knew himself to be in a ticklish situation. He was forced to remain where he was unless he wished to so demean himself as to bellow for help like some calf struck in the briers, yet he could feel it in his bones that whatever Lucy Gladwin was about to say next, it boded no good for him — no good at all.

"Very well, missy," he countered with all the sangfroid he could muster, "you have gained your objective. Perceive me standing here. Now," he ended, straightening once again and directing his eyes meaningfully toward the door, "if that is all you required . . ." His voice trailed off suggestively.

"Oh, how insufferably priggish you can be!" Lucy exclaimed in amused frustration, fairly hopping to her feet. "I don't know why I even bother trying to talk to you. Aunt Rachel says I must have windmills in my head to —"

"Ah, then I was correct in my assessment of that estimable lady. It is a pity you don't strive to emulate her — your brain could do with an infusion of common sense."

Lucy's eyes narrowed to glittering blue slits as she continued recklessly, "You didn't let me finish, my lord. What Aunt Rachel said was that anyone who could see anything more in you other than an overweening conceit and a total contempt for your fellowman should hand himself over to the leeches for a thorough examination. I begin to see the wisdom of her words!"

Thorpe extracted his snuffbox and delicately took a pinch before, dusting his fingertips on his handkerchief, he drawled languidly, "I assume that charming little outburst brings our . . . er . . . *discussion* to a close? One can only hope it likewise heralds the death of your ridiculous puppy love and the cessation of your so fatiguing public displays of affection. A word to the wise, child — gentlemen prefer to do the chasing, not the other way about."

"Oh, *why* do I bother?" Lucy asked the room in general, now genuinely distressed. "You've been so blinded by your rank and position that you refuse to listen to the commands of your own heart. You're not so cold as you try to make people believe, I just know it. But if you don't stop worrying about your *outside* and start listening to your *inside,* you'll never be really happy."

"I'm listening to my *inside* right now, you impertinent creature," he cut in heartlessly, deliberately looking straight into Lucy's tear-drenched eyes, "and it's telling me it wants its luncheon. Now, are you going to open this door or must I be forced to endure more of these childish histrionics? By God, you are the most bold, ill-mannered girl I have ever met. Even as I stand here, I cannot believe we are having this entire conversation."

"You'll be sorry, my lord," Lucy sniffed,

reaching into her bodice and extracting a small brass key. "If you marry for duty, with no thought to what will make you happy, you'll soon turn into the very man my aunt says you are. Please, consider what I'm saying. I know I'm being horribly forward and probably have disgraced myself in your eyes forevermore, but I see goodness in you. I have always seen it. If I can make you listen, all will not have been lost."

"Now she casts herself in the dual role of martyr and savior of my soon-to-be-damned soul. Please, after all I have been forced to endure from you over the years, can you not find it in yourself to spare me from your attempts at salvation!" Thorpe quipped meanly, more angry than he could remember being since . . . He hesitated, finally realizing that he couldn't remember *ever* having been this angry.

Quaking ever so slightly in her slippers as she flinched from the dark look that had settled over the earl's handsome face, Lucy knew she had made a complete shambles of this, their only real conversation in the three years she had known him. And after all her high hopes!

She walked slowly toward the earl, not knowing how appealing she looked

wrapped in the cloak of her hurt and innocence, and placed the key in his waiting
hand. "I beg your forgiveness for having
behaved so badly, my lord. I have been
guilty of many small indiscretions in the
past, but I have really passed beyond the
pale with this last scheme.

"It was only that I was so desperate, you
know, although that certainly is no excuse.
I thought I was trying to help you, but I
see now that my motives were entirely self-
serving. I duped myself, pursuing a dream
that had no basis in reality. You are not the
man I thought you were, for even if you
could not find it in your heart to . . . to like
me, the man I believed you to be could
never have been so consciously cruel.
Good day, my lord. You shall not be forced
to endure my attentions in the future."

Looking up into his closed expression,
she summoned a small brave smile. "See,
my lord. The purpose of your visit has
been accomplished after all — and before
the hall clock could chime the half-hour.
Congratulations."

Unlocking the door, Thorpe held out the
key, but when Lucy just shook her head,
her entire being concentrating on not
bursting into tears and thus losing the last
of her self-respect, he stepped past her to

lay it on a nearby table. He didn't feel particularly proud of himself for this day's work; bludgeoning a mere slip of a girl with his tongue could not be looked upon as the gentlemanly thing to do. But if he had at last destroyed her ridiculous worship of him, convinced her to stop throwing herself in his way and disrupting his peace, he could not help but view his actions as necessary, in the interests of self-preservation at the very least.

"Good day to you, Miss Gladwin. Rest assured this conversation will remain solely between the two of us. There is no need for further hostilities, either privately or in public. A common nod when we meet will be sufficient to keep the tongues from wagging, I believe, and should not cause either of us any undue hardship."

Then, when she made no move to answer him, he did something he later told himself was no more than an impetuous act containing no real meaning: he lifted her hand to his lips, placed a slight kiss on her cool flesh, and then took his leave without a backward glance — leaving Lucy to cradle her hand protectively against her breast as she watched him walk out of her life.

CHAPTER THREE

"Did you hear?"

"It's all over the city!"

"I heard that letters were sent to all the newspapers — it has to be true!"

"Such a scandal! Who would have thought it of him? And what about his poor fiancée? Has anybody seen her? Is he with her, do you think?"

"I cannot believe he'd dare to show his face! Not after what he's done! It's horrid, simply horrid!"

What a to-do! Ever since she and her aunt had set foot inside the ballroom there had been no denying that something was afoot — that some wickedly delicious bit of gossip was being passed around the flower-bedecked room, thoroughly taking the shine out of Miss Araminta Selbridge's debut at her painstakingly planned come-out ball.

The very air crackled with tension as the invited guests forsook the sanded dance floor in favor of standing about in tight little clumps, talking nineteen to the dozen while they gleefully shredded some unfortunate soul's reputation into tiny bits.

After depositing Aunt Rachel with the dowagers, her relative being nearly dragged into a chair beside the turbaned dragon who immediately began wetly whispering into the poor lady's ear, Lucy wandered off aimlessly, forgetting that she had promised to immediately join some young female acquaintances that were standing nearby, deep in frenzied conversation.

More than a week had passed since her disastrous meeting with Lord Thorpe, and although her aunt refused to do as her niece asked and allow them both to quit the city at once, Lucy's heart had not been in any of the parties, fêtes, or routs she had dutifully allowed herself to be dragged off to night after endless night.

She had seen Thorpe twice in that time, and he had made a point of acknowledging her presence even though Lucy had barely responded to his greetings before, shame burning in her hot cheeks as she remembered every scathing word he had said to her, she melted hastily into any nearby group of people or handy quiet anteroom.

Embarrassment played a part in her actions, but not a large one. She had, as she had acknowledged ruefully to her aunt when she confessed her crime, put her foot in it badly this time, but it was her bruised heart that was suffering, and not her pride. She had believed herself truly in love with Julian Rutherford, and even now her illusions about the man, having been struck down most unmercifully by his cruelty and indifference, were not really ready to die.

Waving languidly to several acquaintances who tried to draw her into their conversation, Lucy now contented herself with making a lazy circle of the large room, only idly wondering why no one was dancing. Whatever juicy bit of new gossip had taken their attention, it was still difficult to believe that it could keep the younger members of the party away from the floor when the musicians were playing such a lively tune.

Out of the corners of her eyes Lucy could see her aunt beckoning to her, very determinedly gesturing for her niece to join her at the side of the ballroom. Thinking that perhaps Aunt Rachel could enlighten her as to what was going forward, and not really interested enough to have to winnow out the facts from the extraneous exposition that excited gabble-mongers would generously sprinkle into their version of the scandal, she made for the woman's side and made herself comfortable on one of the fan-backed chairs.

"My goodness, Aunt, have you ever seen anything to match it? Anyone would think Prinny had just announced he was giving up his title to marry a scullery maid. Tell me, what is it you have gleaned?"

Now that she had her niece back at her side, Rachel Gladwin was torn as to exactly what she should do. While part of her wanted to whisk Lucy away before she got wind of what was about and made a cake out of herself in public, another, more realistic part of her knew that the time and place would make little difference to the news she had to impart. It would only be delaying the inevitable.

"It's about Lord Thorpe, dearest," she said at last, uneasily avoiding Lucy's suddenly widened eyes.

"Lord Thorpe ran off with a scullery maid?" Lucy joked, suddenly not wanting to hear the truth.

"If it were only that simple," her aunt sighed, reaching over to hold her niece's kid-encased hand. "I don't know the whole of it yet, so I don't want you screeching out loud or anything when I tell you, do you understand?"

"He . . . he's not . . . *dead?*" Lucy

pleaded in a husky whisper.

"It's worse than that, my precious. They say he's . . . Oh dear, how do I say this to an innocent like you? He's gotten a girl in his home county into a . . . um . . . delicate condition, and left her to do away with herself in despair."

"*What!*" Lucy exploded, causing several of the nearby dowagers to cast curious glances in her direction. "What nonsense!" she hissed, heeding the warning pressure of her aunt's hand. "Only a ninny would believe such a ridiculous thing."

"Be that as it may, Lucy, the facts speak for themselves. I understand there was a note telling all."

"A suicide note?" Lucy asked, still trying to reconcile her image of the man with the thought of Lord Thorpe rolling about in the hay with some village lass. "How has word of such a note gotten all the way from Derbyshire to London?"

While Lucy sat rigidly in her chair, her eyes staring blankly at the people who were busily destroying Lord Thorpe's reputation with their pointed tongues, her aunt outlined what she had heard.

It seemed that there had lived, in a village near Thorpe's estate, a young woman of quality whose family had fallen on hard times. Enter Lord Thorpe, promising marriage and a rescue from penury, and the plot began to thicken. As the story went — and the story had gone very nicely so far, seeing as how the young lady had written it down in all its sordid detail and then posted a copy to each of the London dailies — Lord Thorpe seduced this poor innocent, one Susan Anscom, on the promise of marriage, and then coldly discarded her when she revealed herself to be with child. After pouring out her grief to the gossip rags, the distraught girl had then chosen the only route open to her — she had drowned herself in the village pond.

"Ridiculous!" was all Lucy could respond once her aunt was finished speaking. "Who could ever believe such a bag of moonshine? Lord Thorpe would never sink to such a thing — he's too much the gentleman, for one thing. Besides," she added matter-of-factly, "he'd never stoop to consorting with any woman ranked lower than someone like Lady Cynthia." Raising her eyes to scan the room, she wondered aloud, "Where *is* Lady Cynthia? I thought I saw her father going into one of the card rooms earlier. Could it be she is circulating about the room defending her betrothed against such evil lies?"

Rachel looked about the ballroom, locating Lady Cynthia as she stood talking to a group of people who seemed to be hanging on her every word. "There she is, Lucy," she said as she pointed discreetly in that general direction, "standing beside Lord Seabrook. My goodness, she seems to be laughing. How can she be so unaffected by all of this?"

Lucy paused a moment in her worry over Lord Thorpe to give herself a mental kick for being so unkind to Lady Cynthia in the past. Obviously the woman was putting a brave face on this, acting as if nothing had happened, and circulating throughout the room explaining away any questions anyone might have.

"But where is Lord Thorpe?" her aunt went on to question when Lucy said nothing. "Surely he has accompanied her here this evening? They never go anywhere except together." Rachel blushed a bit, adding, "I'm sorry, pet, but over the past three years you have made me quite an authority on his lordship and his movements."

There was a sudden commotion at the doorway, releasing Lucy from giving some sort of answer to her aunt, and all heads turned in time to see Lord Thorpe enter the ballroom. He looked, as was his custom, magnificent. From his finely arranged blond locks to the tips of his shiny evening slippers, he was every inch the complete gentleman. Lucy's heart, always fickle when she counted on it for steadiness, did a little flip-flop in her breast as she drank in his handsomeness and the flagrantly arrogant stare he took up as he stopped to survey the room through his quizzing glass.

Spotting his fiancée at the far end of the floor, he began a leisurely progress down the room, and it wasn't until he was three-quarters of the way to his destination that he realized all conversation had stopped and he was the object of every eye in the place. Even the musicians had ceased their frantic fiddling meant to entice somebody out on the floor before Araminta Selbridge's papa refused to pay them for their night's work.

Turning slowly on his heels, Lord Thorpe looked back to see that all those he had already passed by were now standing with their backs turned against him. His spine stiffening perceptibly, he turned forward once again and, glancing neither right nor left, resumed his journey to his fiancée's side. As he walked on, one by one the guests he passed lifted their noses and pointedly turned their backs on him, until, when he reached the group he sought and prepared to bow, Lady Cynthia slipped a gloved hand into the crook of Lord Seabrook's arm and led her friends in a short procession that left them facing a potted plant in a corner of the room.

"They're cutting him!" Lucy burst out indignantly. "The bloody fools are cutting him dead! And to think I had for a moment believed that mean cat was human after all! *How dare she!*"

"Lucy," her aunt pleaded in an undertone, "please keep your voice down. Lord Thorpe will withdraw shortly and then we may quit this den of fools, but for the moment I can only implore you not to do anything you may regret. His lordship wouldn't thank you for it, you know."

Tears of mingled pity and frustration glittering in her eyes, Lucy could not tear her gaze away from the confused man who now stood looking about him dazedly, his broad shoulders slumped in defeat. He, a man who prided himself on his fine reputation, he, the leader of the small, select circle that he had for so many years ruled by means of his impeccable taste, exalted lineage, and impressive appearance, had just cruelly learned the true nature of his contemporaries. He was, to say the thing plainly, shocked spitless.

The nervous musicians, not knowing what else to do, struck up a waltz, thinking to fill the great void of silence with some soothing music. No one moved. Like statues carved from cold marble, the lords and ladies of the *ton* were waiting for the untouchable who had lately been their leader to take his offending self off so that they might not be exposed to his presence. Mud sticks, his former friends were well aware, and they were making sure to cut a wide berth around the man lest some of his dirt leap onto their spotless reputations.

Lucy took it for as long as she could (approximately ten seconds, eight of them spent disengaging her aunt's clinging hands) before rising to scamper hurriedly down the long room to tug at his lordship's sleeve. "Lord Thorpe!" she declared loudly. "I was so worried you had forgotten, but I can see you are a man of your word. Here you are, just as the dance you had me reserve for you is about to begin. I'm sorry you couldn't find me at once; I was bearing my aunt company with the dowagers while waiting for you." Sliding her gloved hand around his sleeve, she smiled up at him, hiding the fact that her slim fingers were crushing his arm in silent warning. "Shall we, my lord?" she asked, steel in her voice, and the shattered, confused man at last responded, leading her out onto the floor.

They were, of course, the only dancers on the floor, and all eyes were on the couple that now waltzed around the room that suddenly seemed as wide and as dangerous as a battlefield. "Don't look now, my lord," Lucy told him, still maintaining her bright smile, "but Lady Fairweather, known to you formerly as Lady Cynthia, is making a great show of laughing at something that vile Lord Seabrook has whispered in her traitorous ear."

As her partner's only response was to grip her hand tighter, she went on, "Dance me over to the doorway, my lord, and we shall waltz our way out of this gathering of traitors. Only hold on a while longer, please, and we shall get you out of this yet with a whole skin."

Julian looked down on her imploring face with eyes that seemed curiously dead. His feet continued to move in the familiar waltz steps; his heart, he noticed randomly, continued to beat on in his numb body, so how could it be that he felt he had just lost all control over his own destiny? One moment he had been Julian Rutherford, Earl of Thorpe, and he thought without conceit, master of all he surveyed; and the next, he had been struck from his position of majesty, owing the fact that he even remained upright to the small girl he now clung to with the remaining vestiges of his strength.

Out of the corners of her eyes Lucy could see her Aunt Rachel standing just inside the main doorway, a footman bearing their evening cloaks hovering at her side. Good old Rachel, she rejoiced silently, I knew I could count on her to keep her head. Aloud, she soothed, "It's nearly over, my lord, you're holding up just fine. Only whirl me about a time or two, as sort of a farewell flourish — just to let these low-lifes know we don't give a fig for what they think."

Julian, who had for three-and-thirty years subscribed to Fielding's definition of the word "nobody" as meaning "all the people in Great Britain except about twelve hundred," and the word "world" as being "your own acquaintance," could not as easily dismiss the evident condemnation of his peers. His whole life had been crumbling around his feet ever since he'd first realized that no one, not even his fiancée, was going to stand behind him in his time of trouble, and his only ally was to be a young slip of a girl. The same girl he had cut from his life so ruthlessly not a fortnight before.

"Why are you doing this?" he asked now in a strangled voice.

Lucy's bright smile blazed up at him before she replied confidently, "Because I'm a bloody fool, my lord. Why else?"

Lucy and Rachel were up at the crack of dawn the next morning, setting the kitchen staff at sixes and sevens with their requests for an early breakfast, while the third underfootman was not best pleased to be ordered out into the streets to procure copies of every newspaper in the city.

Two of the papers had declined to run the story sent to them by one Susan Anscom, but a third, less scrupulous publication (or perhaps less indebted monetarily to Lord Thorpe) printed the entire letter on the first inside page.

It was a thoroughly damning epitaph, set forth with a thoroughness not usually looked for in hysterical females. The missive detailed her seduction at the hands of

Lord T—, her inevitable pregnancy, and that same man's callous indifference to her plight. It recounted how she planned, presumably after posting her condemnation, to fling herself into the small pond behind her home in Alsop-en-le-Dale, a scant four miles from Lord T—'s country home, an action she did in fact take, according to the newspaper report. The story ended with the intelligence that Miss Anscom's suicide had "put a period to her young life and set loose the biggest scandal in many a year."

As if the article by itself were not enough, the footman also produced a few assorted caricatures from local print shops, where patrons could buy ludicrous drawings depicting Lord T— either standing with his heel crushing the head of some helpless infant, departing on horseback while an obviously increasing damsel stares distractedly into a becoming pool of water, or one particularly repulsive colored print (which cost all of a guinea, but with the ladies footing the bill, it seemed a small expenditure) that showed Lord T— actually stuffing Miss A— into a sack in preparation for tossing her into the water. This last print Rachel wisely kept from Lucy's sight.

"How dare they lampoon him like this!"

Lucy protested, ripping one of the cartoons into small pieces.

"If Prinny himself is not safe from such attack, my dear, I doubt Lord Thorpe can be considered above it," Rachel answered, shaking her head. "I can only wonder how Lord Thorpe is taking it. The story must have been fairly well spread last night for society to have already mounted a snub of such proportions. But now, now that every man on the street has been made aware of it, there's no telling what will happen next. Poor man," she ended, taking a sip of chocolate. "Poor, proud man."

Lucy sat back against her chair, her blue eyes clouded by the memory of Lord Thorpe as she had last seen him outside the Selbridge mansion. Standing ramrod straight, his wide mouth set in a thin line, he had thanked his rescuer with formal politeness before stepping into his waiting coach and driving away without a backward glance. The fact that he had neglected to see that the Gladwin carriage had been called for or wait until such time as it had arrived fairly screamed out his distraction.

"I should think he would like nothing more than to sit in some dark room and cry his eyes out," Lucy said now, wiping away a tear of her own. "He has been totally devastated by this thing. It is terrible to watch the mighty fall. Lord Thorpe has no experience of failure, you know. He has lived his life within a charmed circle. But now he knows how false his life has been and he cannot cope."

"Oh, Lucy, I think you might be overstating the case," her aunt contradicted weakly. "Surely not all the *ton* have turned their backs on the man. Why, I wager that by this morning he has found that many friends have rallied around him. Surely it is all a nine days' wonder, and the whole matter will be forgotten by next week."

"Really, Aunt? And they say I am an optimist!" Lucy stood up in preparation for leaving the sun-drenched dining room. "Well, one thing is for certain. *I* shall not leave him to face this morning's news alone. Aunt? Are you coming with me, or are you afraid to be seen entering his lordship's place of residence for fear of being tarred with the same brush?"

Laying down her fork, giving one long, wistful look at the curried eggs Cook had concocted just for her, Rachel rose and followed her niece out of the room. "I should have said yes to Lord Manton," she remarked to no one in particular. "Marriage

58

to that wet-palmed man would have been tedious, but at least it would have been peaceful."

If Lucy Gladwin thought that Julian Rutherford was spending his morning sobbing into his porridge, she was fair and far out in her judgment of the man. Oh yes, he had been more than a little overset at the Selbridges' when he found himself on the receiving end of an *en masse* cut direct, but he had no intention of slitting his wrists over the affair. There had to have been some mistake, that was all. A few hotheads, a few eager gossip-mongers, had succeeded in stirring up a tempest in a teapot. It would soon blow over, once his friends realized that he, Lord Thorpe, was not only too gentlemanly ever to lie to a woman, but too fastidious to bestow his favors randomly upon females not schooled in preventing what would otherwise be the inevitable outcome of such activities.

Why, at any minute his butler would enter the room to announce the arrival of friends come to support him in his hour of need. Hadn't he dressed and made himself available to callers on the basis of just this assumption? It was of no real consequence that Lord Royston, Lord Storm, the Earl of Lockport, the Duke of Avonall, and several other of his cronies were at the moment deep in Sussex at a house party — there were others he knew he could count on to rally to his side. Ah, ha! There went the door knocker just now! Patting down his already perfect cravat, Lord Thorpe rose to receive the first caller come to declare himself an ally.

"Miss Rachel Gladwin and Miss Lucille Gladwin, my lord," the butler intoned solemnly before bowing the two ladies into the drawing room and withdrawing to finish the letter he had been penning to his cousin, majordomo to a duke, requesting his aid in obtaining a position for him in a less-tainted domicile.

"How can we help?" Lucy said baldly, not wasting precious time with formalities.

"I don't think you can," Lord Thorpe replied tonelessly, rather deflated by the thought that so far the only troops that had rallied to his cause were wearing petticoats.

"Oh, come now, my lord," Lucy admonished as she sat herself down on a nearby chair. "All is not so black as you may think. Have you no touch of spunk?"

"If you mean, have I yet ordered a length of rope sufficient for hanging myself from the chandelier in the foyer, no, I have not sunk that far," he returned, his upper lip curling just a little bit.

Lucy turned to her aunt, just now sinking into a chair set away from the center of the room, hoping to fade into the background. "See, Aunt Rachel, it's just as I told you. The man lives on his pride. Just like Mr. Darcy in Miss Austen's *Pride and Prejudice*. Of course," she added, looking back at her unwilling host, "he isn't quite the right coloring, is he? But no matter. It is much the same thing in the end. Mr. Darcy learned that pride has its price and overcame *his* failings."

When it looked as if Lucy was about to gift him with a synopsis of the plot of the novel that had just lately been published in the metropolis, he cut in, saying, "In my heart of hearts I'm *sure* there is a reason for this visit, ladies, or at least I devoutly hope so. I regret that I shambled off so abruptly last evening, but you must understand that I was preoccupied with a personal matter. If I did not thank you sufficiently for your assistance at the time, I will try to remedy that lapse now."

"Oh, cut line, my lord," Lucy interrupted, wrinkling her nose at his fustiness. "We all can read, you know, and I doubt calling Susan Anscom's suicide a personal matter will wrest her story from the lips of every muckraking busybody in town. No, what we must do is defang the vipers."

"We?" his lordship repeated heavily. "I was not of the opinion that I had requested you or anyone else to become a martyr in my cause. Besides, what makes you think I would want your help?"

"Indeed," Aunt Rachel piped up from her corner of the room. "Seeing as how the place is already littered thick with those wishing to spring to your defence." Her small bit said, she closed her mouth and sat back to see if her little stab had pricked his lordship's arrogant demeanor.

The silence in the room following Rachel's blunt declaration was almost as ominous as the dark expression that had descended on the earl's fair features. Lucy could feel a slight prickle of nervousness creeping up her spine, and she wasn't even the target of his piercing gaze. But when Rachel kept her eyes averted, calmly running her gloves through her fingers, he realized that, facetious though her remark might have been, there was a germ of truth in what she said.

He walked over to the bell-pull and summoned a servant, requesting refreshments be brought immediately, and then sat himself down in a seat across from the one Lucy had taken up when she came into the room. "All right, ladies," he conceded in rare good humor, "you have made your point. However, I still fail to see why you are here. Especially," he added more softly, "considering the shabby treatment you have lately suffered at my hands."

Smiling broadly at his lordship's admission that his handling of their recent confrontation had been shabby in the extreme, Lucy decided once again that her reading of her beloved's character had not been in error. "Why, we are here to tell you that we don't believe a word of this nonsense about you and Miss Anscom," she told him fiercely. "And to offer our services, of course."

"Your services for what?" Lord Thorpe was moved to ask, still trying to shake the feeling that he was lost in the middle of a nightmare and showing no signs of waking up in the near future.

Lucy leaned forward conspiratorially and said grimly, "I have given this a good deal of thought since last night. I feel this whole thing is a plot to rob you of your good name and drive you distracted into an early grave."

"Oh, I seriously doubt that," Julian replied, biting back a laugh at the sight of Lucy's intense expression.

"No, really," she assured him, shifting so that she sat perched right on the edge of her chair. "Only think how thorough this Miss Anscom was — writing to all the papers."

"Hmm," he mused back at her, "and then drowning herself in the village pond just to lend credence to her story. I must agree, the woman certainly *was* thorough."

Now Lucy supplied the coup de grace. "My Lord Thorpe, how deep is the village pond?"

"I haven't the faintest idea. It is certainly not a big body of water."

"Exactly! The pond near our home is no more than three or four feet deep, even in the center. I imagine Miss Anscom's pond to be about the same depth. If she did indeed drown, as the newspaper says it has confirmed, I find it mind-boggling to understand how she could have had such perseverance — holding her own head beneath the surface for the length of time required."

Lord Thorpe jumped to his feet, two high spots of color in his cheeks. "This is how you're going to help me? By spreading about the insinuation that I've *murdered* this Miss Anscom? A little more 'help' from you, madam, and I shan't have to go to the trouble of purchasing my own rope!"

CHAPTER FOUR

It did precious little to relieve Lord Thorpe's uneasy mind that Lucy Gladwin had been the only visitor ushered into his drawing room in the two interminable days following his embarrassment at the Selbridge ball. He was so alone in his misery, in fact, that he had almost begun to regret the fact that he had, at the time of that visit, come within amesace of tossing that same Lucy Gladwin out onto the flagway on her dainty little ear.

"I *am* getting desperate," he told himself ruefully as he slouched inelegantly in a chair in his private sanctum, his book-lined study at the rear of the Thorpe mansion. "Anyone who would feel the least pang at the absence of that outrageous little baggage has got to be desperate. Or else," he muttered, looking owlishly into the near-empty brandy snifter he held in his hand, "well and truly corned, which I do believe I am."

Poor, poor Lord Thorpe. He was truly a man alone, with his only company the half-dozen decanters of fine old brandy he had been consuming steadily ever since bolting himself inside his study the previous morning. His fine clothing, donned the day before in anticipation of putting on a brave front for his supporters as they rallied around him, was now sadly crushed and dotted with brandy stains — and perhaps a tear stain or two?

That he had dealt so cavalierly with the one supporter who had braved society to comfort him he reconciled to the fact that the dratted chit had, while supposedly lending him solace, damn near come out and accused him of murder!

"Perhaps it is better I am alone," he told a bust of Nelson that sat in a niche across the room. "Many more like her and I'll find myself in Old Bailey fighting for my life." The admiral only stared off into the distance with his one good eye, refusing, so it seemed, to acknowledge his lordship's scandal-tainted presence.

His lordship's servants had been cutting a wide berth around him, but had delivered to him the small box that had arrived earlier by messenger, a box containing the Rutherford ancestral betrothal ring and nothing else. After Lady Cynthia's behavior when last he saw her, Julian had not been too surprised, although her action had not measurably enhanced his opinion of women, which had never had much reason to be more than it should be.

Tossing off the remainder of his drink, he thought fleetingly of his mama, the grande dame who had been the first to impress on him the honor and duty attached to being born a Rutherford. That she was for the moment in the far reaches of Scotland, dutifully burying a distant relative (and sniffing about for any bit of inheritance that might come her way), could only be considered a gift from the gods, for the old lady would have murdered him for allowing his good name to be dragged in the mire in this tacky way.

"Here's to you, Mama," the earl quipped, holding out his empty snifter and then dashing it to the hearth. "You taught me everything I needed to know about being a titled gentleman. 'Tis a great, bleeding pity you didn't teach me how fickle it all can be."

He stood and walked to the fireplace to inspect the damage he had wrought and found it to be depressingly insufficient. Turning back to face his desk, he swept the pile of tradesmen's bills from the surface with one angry swipe of his arm. "The meanest cut of all," he observed feelingly as he watched the papers flutter about the room before settling on the floor. That the common man had felt the need to call in their bills showed just how far his disgrace had plunged his good name.

But if he had thought he was already as low as a man could go, the note his butler brought him a few minutes later showed him that he had no idea of the thoroughness of his fall from grace. Clutching the note in his fist, he called for a servant to send word to have his closed carriage brought round immediately.

And as he gave his coachman Lucy Gladwin's direction, he took the first step into becoming the man Lucy had thought him to be all along.

"I despair of ever making him understand," Lucy said gloomily as she sat in the morning room, her embroidery lying forgotten in her lap. "When I think of how . . . *overset* . . . Lord Thorpe was when I mentioned that bit about the pond, I cannot help but despair of his *ever* listening to reason while there is still time to help him."

Lucy's audience of one — her long-suffering Aunt Rachel (who had been hearing this sad refrain for the past four-

and-twenty hours) — now replied evenly, "A bit more 'despair,' pet, and I shall begin to believe it is *you* who are going into a sad decline, and not Lord Thorpe. Really, my dear, I think you refine too much on this murder theory of yours. This is just another garden-variety *ton* scandal, and will blow over by next week."

"I think not, Aunt!" Lucy returned earnestly. "A scandal of these proportions does not blow away like a puff of smoke. Oh no! Mark my words — I smell a deep intrigue here, I'm sure of it."

"You scent a chance to endear yourself to Lord Thorpe while that man is vulnerable to an assault on his tender feelings, you mean," her aunt contradicted without rancor. "You may hoodwink others with that wide-eyed look of innocence, missy, but you're wasting your efforts in trying to convince *this* particular audience of your selflessness."

"Oh, pooh!" Lucy tossed out lightheartedly. "I never said I didn't hope to take advantage of this chance to alert Julian to my finer qualities. But I do mean it when I say I think he is in real danger. Someone went to a lot of trouble to launch this scandal, and I can't make myself believe simple mischief was the motivation."

"The Earl of Thorpe, ma'am," the butler intoned in a suitably awed voice from the doorway, then stood aside as his lordship lurched past him into the room.

Lucy could not help the involuntary gasp of incredulity that escaped her lips at the sight of the disheveled earl. He looked, so she thought, as if he had just come off the loser in a heated battle, and she could only stare at his unshaven face and red-rimmed eyes.

"My lord," Rachel said calmly, indicating a nearby chair, which Julian dropped into gratefully. "Biggs," she said in an aside to the gape-mouthed butler, "I do believe we should like a pot of coffee as soon as possible. A rather *large* pot, actually."

"Oh, I knew it! *I just knew it would come to this!*" Lucy exclaimed, rushing to shut the door on Biggs's departing back. "They're after you, aren't they?"

"Who's after me?" the earl questioned, staring at Lucy owlishly as that female threw her back against the closed doors as if to ward off an imminent invasion.

"The constable! The Bow Street Runners! The *law!*"

"It pains me to disappoint you, brat," the earl said, regaining a bit of his dignity, and

71

with it his sarcastic wit. "I am not, alas, in imminent danger of being clapped into irons and hauled off to jail. However, if you wish me to send one of the servants round to Bethlehem Hospital, I'm sure you'd find sufficient drama in having your own private piece of Bedlam to call your own. Really, Miss Gladwin, you must learn to control these wild flights of imagination. I do believe such transports may be injurious to your spleen or something."

Rachel choked delicately into her handkerchief as Lucy, her expression suitably chastened, returned slowly to her seat, at last ready to listen to what his lordship had to say. "Pardon me, my lord," she begged, her lower lip trembling appealingly. "I let my fears run away with me for a moment there, didn't I? But you look so . . . that is to say, you are not looking yourself . . . not that you don't look fine as ninepence, you understand . . . but . . . but . . ."

"I apologize for burdening you both with my outlandish appearance, for there is no need to dress it up in fine linen — I look like a common ruffian and I know it. I don't know exactly why I am here, to tell the God's truth, except that I could not think of any other door in all of London that would be open to me."

His little bit of humble pie swallowed, Lord Thorpe leaned heavily against the back of his chair and stared at the crumpled piece of paper he still held tight in his hand. "They've asked me to resign from my club," he muttered half under his breath. "Six generations of Rutherfords have been members. My disgrace is now total."

While some females may not have understood the gravity of this last snub delivered to Lord Thorpe by his contemporaries, Lucy Gladwin, who had been raised by a worldly-wise father, immediately recognized that the worst, the absolute *worst* had happened. "Oh, you *poor thing!*" she exclaimed, dropping to her knees at his feet.

Biggs interrupted the proceedings at that moment, bringing in the coffee tray — which might have been a good thing, for Lord Thorpe, at Lucy's show of sympathy, was perilously near to unmanning himself in the company of females, a truly unpardonable breach of gentlemanly behavior. Rising to walk over to a nearby window, pretending to look out over the rear garden until he could regain control of his emotions, he waited until the door had closed behind the butler before turning to face the women. "I . . . I'm sorry, ladies. It seems such a piddling thing, doesn't it, when compared to the rest? But somehow . . . somehow —"

"Mr. Dexter Rutherford," Biggs proclaimed, excitement evident in his voice as a dazzling young Tulip of Fashion brushed past him to stand in the middle of the morning room, quizzing glass stuck to his eye.

"I say, Julian, your man was right," the young exquisite remarked after bowing to the ladies. "Strange sort of bolt hole, I thought at the time, right here smack in the center of Mayfair, but then I said to myself, where else could Cousin Julian go? Surely not to Piccadilly!"

The earl looked at his cousin, his expression more pained than angry. "I trust you will explain that remark, Dexter."

Crossing his legs carefully after making much ado about the spreading of his coattails before sitting himself down in the most comfortable chair in the room, Mr. Rutherford expanded graciously, "I was on the hunt for you this morning, of course. I had to listen to a load of drivel from your butler — the man has handed in his notice, by the by, seeing as how he cannot allow his name to be linked with yours now that you are fallen so low — who told me you had hightailed it over here like some madman, without even lingering long enough to change your linen. I see the man was correct," he ended, looking his cousin up and down and shaking his head in sorrow. "God man, can anything be that bad, that you would run about in your dirt for all the world and his wife to see you?"

"They've asked him to resign from his club," Rachel put in softly, content to sit back and watch events as they unfolded, only tossing in a word or two at appropriate times to keep the thing lively.

"Oh, that's too bad of them!" Dexter commiserated feelingly. "Though I imagine they'd do much the same to me, except that in the clubs I frequent, such notoriety would probably get me a free round of drinks!"

Lucy, who had been in deep thought ever since Dexter's name had been announced, finally spoke. "They're after you too, aren't they, Dex? And it's that, and not cousinly concern, that has you flying over here this morning."

Dexter flashed his cousin an insouciant smile. "Sharp as a tack, ain't she, coz? Like Lucy excessively, you know, always have. But she's right, of course. You know, when I first heard of your plight I thought, couldn't happen to a nicer, more deserving bloke. The whole thing, actually, would have been ever so amusing except that now the world has got the needle into *me* — seeing as how I'm living on m'expectations. Only stands to reason — if you go down, your heir goes right along with you. I should think you would have considered me a little bit before tumbling the chit. Poor sporting of you, Julian, it really was."

A sound much resembling a low animal growl issued from his lordship's throat as he made to throttle the handsome blond, slim, younger version of himself as that gentleman stepped swiftly to stand behind Lucy's chair seeking petticoat protection in hopes it would save him from a bloody nose.

"Now, now, my lord," Lucy intervened, rising to her feet and putting out her hands in warning (and barely hiding the smile that lurked at the corners of her mouth). "You can't blame poor Dex for feeling sadly used. Just think — all his props have just been cut out from under him, and when he runs to his beloved cousin for guidance, he finds you wallowing so deeply in your own self-pity that it is no wonder his tact has gone a-begging."

"His *wits* have gone a-begging," the earl

contradicted meanly. "I never thought my own flesh and blood would believe these calumnies broadcast against me."

"Oh, he doesn't really believe them," Lucy explained. "It's just that he's upset."

"I don't? I am?" Mr. Rutherford ventured confusedly. "That is to say, of course I don't! How could I believe such a thing of Julian? After all he's an arrogant bas— that is to say, a high stickler, he's a good old fellow for all that. Towed me out of River Tick more than once, as a matter of fact. I was merely overcome for a moment, wasn't I, Lucy?"

"Exactly." Lucy nodded emphatically, changing a look out of the corners of her eyes to see that his lordship, only slightly mollified but still very weary, had subsided once more into his chair.

"If I were an enterprising sort of female," Rachel remarked to no one in particular, "I should be out in the square selling tickets to this circus. Lucy," she prompted, deciding to stir the pot a bit more, "why don't you tell Mr. Rutherford your theory about this whole thing being a conspiracy to have Lord Thorpe sent to the gallows."

Lucy's eyelids narrowed as she assessed the young man. She had been looking about for a likely suspect behind the plot, and Dexter Rutherford, next in line to the peerage, seemed as good a place as any to start. "I don't think it wise to discuss strategy with our prime suspect, Aunt Rachel," she intoned heavily.

Dexter looked about the room, realizing that he had suddenly become the center of some decidedly hostile attention. "Plot? What plot? Who's a suspect? *Me?* I didn't do anything. I haven't the brains, for one thing." He turned and spread his arms imploringly in his cousin's direction. "Tell her, Julian. Tell her what a slow-top I am. You know I couldn't be guilty. *Tell her!*"

Julian rubbed a hand across his burning eyes. "He's right, Miss Gladwin," he sighed, shaking his head. "At least he's smart enough to know he's stupid, if that can be any solace to his mama, for it surely is not to me. Relax, Dex, I'm not about to call you out."

"Or cut off my allowance?" the semi-relieved young man pursued.

"Or cut off your allowance," the earl agreed, silently wondering as to the future of the Rutherford line if Dexter *were* to become the next Earl of Thorpe. The resulting mental picture lent new resolve to his flagging spirits. "But I think I can no longer brush off Miss Gladwin's theory. Someone has gone to a lot of trouble to discredit me. The next logical step would be to prove me criminally as well as morally corrupt."

"I say, Julian, that's coming on a bit strong, isn't it? I mean, all you did was disappoint some country female. How was you to know she'd be such a gudgeon as to go jumping in the pond like some penny-press looby? It's not that you wouldn't have provided for the child. You *were* planning to, weren't you?"

"You idiot!" the earl exploded, causing his cousin once more to take refuge behind Lucy. "Try to get this through your thick skull — *I did not get Miss Anscom pregnant!* I didn't even *know* the lady!" After taking a deep, steadying breath, he continued: "The entire scandal has been made up out of whole cloth to discredit me. Try, if you can, Dexter, to see me as innocent. I assure you that I am."

"All right, cousin," Mr. Rutherford owned after indulging in a few moments' deep thought — a feat that brought a pain to his temples and made him wish he'd gone to Gentleman Jackson's like he'd planned instead of coming to Portman Square to confront his erring relative. "But the fact remains that Miss Anscom, whether you say you knew her or not — by the by, was that in the ordinary or the biblical sense?" As Lord Thorpe's left eyebrow was developing a warning twitch, he ended that line of thought and pressed on: "This Miss Anscom, lying though she may have been, is *dead,* Julian. If she didn't drown herself over you — whom did she do it over, or because of, or . . . oh, you know what I mean."

"Or did she drown herself at all?" Lucy added, crossing her arms over her bosom and making quite a business out of assembling her features in a judgelike expression of solemn inquiry. "Perhaps the lady had help?"

"*Murder?*" Dexter hissed audibly. "You mean the woman was murdered?"

"Exactly!" Lucy said authoritatively.

Dexter gnawed on his knuckle for a full minute while the others in the room awaited his opinion. At last he raised his head, a slow smile spreading on his vacantly handsome face. "If they hang you, coz, can I still be earl?"

Rachel Gladwin hadn't been so diverted in years, and living with a madcap like her niece Lucy — that was taking into consideration a *lot* of diverting circumstances! After pulling the usually unflappable Lord Thorpe off his cowering cousin before any lasting damage could be inflicted, Rachel had taken charge, sending Mr. Rutherford off with a maid to have his bruised nose attended to, Lord Thorpe was off to his mansion to refresh himself before joining them again in an hour, and Lucy off to her room to do whatever it was Lucy was clearly set to do.

By the time the small party had reassembled in the drawing room, Lucy's intentions were clear. She took center stage immediately, only bowing to Lord Thorpe as that belatedly composed man sat glaring at her, clearly wondering how he had chanced to land amidst this gathering of fools. Dexter, seated at a comforting distance from his cousin, and dabbing quite obviously at his oozing left nostril with his lace handkerchief, was all ears as he waited for Lucy to speak, while Rachel, again seated a little away from the rest, took up her tatting and appeared unconcerned.

"Now that we have all had time to compose ourselves," Lucy began, shooting warning glances at both the Rutherfords, "I think we should review what we know and set about formulating a plan of action."

That was as far as Lord Thorpe let Lucy go before breaking in with a word or two of his own. Rising to his full height, his dignity as well as his toilette apparently repaired, he began, "I apologize for bursting in on you ladies this morning. My only excuse is a combination of too little sleep and too many bottles of brandy. I despise myself for my weakness and am here to offer my abject apologies."

Lucy could only smile as she looked at the earl. Even when he groveled, he looked and acted like a king. "Please do not apologize, my lord," she interrupted when it looked as if he were about to launch into a lengthy recitation of his sins. "We are flattered that you trusted us enough to come to us."

The earl bowed slightly, then resumed his rigid stance. "Does not the fact that I had nowhere else to turn dampen your enthusiasm even slightly?"

"I say, coz," Dexter ventured, seeing the sadness flicker in Lucy's eyes, "can't you unbend enough to thank the girl properly? God knows I'm not sure I would have let you across *my* threshold."

The earl had the good grace to look ashamed of himself, a thing Rachel found to be as disconcerting as it was out of character. It would be a pity if Lord Thorpe was drawn to Lucy like a waif seeking comfort — for what would happen to her poor niece once the man no longer needed her? "We are only doing the Christian thing," she pointed out quickly. "Lucy also has a penchant for stray dogs."

Rachel's words served to put his lordship back on his mettle. "I am no stray dog, madam," he informed Rachel coldly. "I was merely trying to explain my vulnerability, which, upon reflection, was highly exaggerated by my shock at being turned on so decisively by my peers. Your niece, in my confusion, seemed like the safest port in my personal storm. However, now that I have my wits about me once again, I have returned to Portman Square only to apologize and to collect my cousin. Dexter?" he ended, gesturing to the comfortably reclining youth to stand and follow him out the door.

"Rather not be seen with you at the moment, cousin," Dexter drawled, raising his index finger to tenderly stroke his abused nose. "Much as this hurts, you seemed almost human when you were knocking me down. Now you're back to being an insufferable prig, I don't believe I care so much for you. Besides, have you forgotten Lucy's theory? Seems to me we'd better put our heads together before you're carted off to jail."

"Are you insinuating that I cannot straighten out this misunderstanding on my own?" the earl questioned, now definitely up on his high ropes. "Moreover, are you really of the opinion that, if I should require assistance, although I do not believe I have alluded to any such eventuality, I would be desperate enough to enlist a young female and a disloyal idiot into my plans?"

Dexter grinned brightly. "Yes, and yes again, coz. You need us, you know, much as the thought must bring you pain."

"Exactly!" Lucy applauded, running over to give Dexter a quick hug. "I have been giving this thing a great deal of thought ever since you left, my lord, and I have decided that the only thing we can do is to adjourn to your home and investigate the business where it first began. Now that Dexter has volunteered —" she eyed the young exquisite owlishly "— you did volunteer, didn't you — I think we shouldn't waste any more time before setting off."

"There is not the smallest need —" Thorpe began before Lucy cut him off by means of a very unladylike snort of disbelief.

"There is *every* need, my lord," she countered, raising her hands to begin ticking off her reasons on her fingers. "One, you cannot just go round bullying the villagers into talking to you about this Miss Anscom. Two, you need a reason to be leaving town in the first place, unless you wish it bandied about that you have been disgraced, jilted, and forced to flee with your tail between your legs. For that reason we will appear to be your guests at a house party that has been planned this age or more. Three, since you are the supposed guilty party, you must be seen to have the support of two London ladies of quality as well as that of your heir. Four, although you are a highly intelligent man, you don't possess the deviousness required to obtain information from unwilling witnesses, or the approachable appearance that is needed to have people confide in you. Five —"

"Enough!" the earl allowed, holding up his hand to stop her. "I'll admit to requiring a bit of assistance. I'll accept Dexter's offer with thanks. But I draw the line at dragging you two ladies into the matter. What sort of gentleman would open two innocent females up to conjecture and censure — being seen with a man so sunk in disgrace."

"A desperate gentleman?" Dexter offered, giving voice to the obvious.

The argument went on at some length — and with some heat — while Rachel sat in her chair and tatted, looking up only sporadically to make sure no one was about to resort to physical violence. For Lord Thorpe had lost his temper as only a very controlled, usually coldly common-sensical person can do, and it would not have surprised the lady if he were soon to begin throwing things.

"You poor abused man, don't you see you need help?" Lucy cried at one point.

"I am not your 'poor man,' madam," he shot back. "And I'm not likely to become an abused anything!"

"Oh, give over, Julian," Dexter needled. "You know less about sleuthing than you do about fuzzing cards. Come down from that tower you live in and face facts — all your money and title and grand old name will get you is cleaner straw in your cell."

On and on it went, well into the afternoon, until finally, possibly only to gain for himself a moment's peace, the earl at last agreed to the plan. They would depart for Thorpe two days hence, taking Parker Rutherford, his distant cousin and personal secretary, along as well.

"I don't see why we need that cawker," Dexter snapped irritably, not knowing well enough to quit while he was ahead. "Talk about your prunes and prisms."

"Parker is also a Rutherford, and it's his good name as well that is being dragged through the mud," Thorpe pointed out. Turning to Lucy, he said, in order to make himself completely clear, "Remember, if you please, that I've only agreed to any of this to clear my family name. None of this is for myself."

"Of course it isn't," his cousin gibed meanly. "You always wanted a longer neck. All the better for tying a neat cravat, what?"

"Will you be putting a notice in the papers — about the house party, I mean," Lucy asked quickly, as a deep red flush crept up his lordship's neck. "I saw the announcement that Lady Cynthia's father inserted this morning of your engagement coming to an end."

Bringing up that particular betrayal dampened Thorpe's rage and sent him plummeting forthwith back into melancholy. His heart was not broken — he couldn't and wouldn't deceive himself on that head — but his pride had taken a mighty blow with Lady Cynthia's defection. A notice of a house party with Miss Lucy Gladwin as his female guest would go a long way in getting some of his own back — considering his former fiancée's outrage at the mere mention of Lucy's name. "I'll see to it that Parker sends it off at once," he told her, his small smile going unnoticed by everyone except Rachel, who missed little.

Once Lord Thorpe had taken his leave and Lucy and Dexter had gone off to put their heads together planning strategy like two generals about to take to the battle-field — or two nursery brats consulting over their toy soldiers — Rachel retired to her room to pen a letter to her brother. Sir Hale may have put her in charge of his volatile daughter, but she wasn't about to bear the brunt of this one on her own. Oh no, brother Hale was to be ordered to send in reinforcements on this one. If he couldn't be trusted to keep Lucy from the briers, at least Rachel wasn't going to be the only one to take the blame. After all, the wisest general knew it paid to cover her flanks!

CHAPTER FIVE

The morning dawned bright and clear, a perfect day for traveling. By nine of the clock four carriages were well on their way north of London, loaded top, back, and sides with strapped-on luggage. Postilions rode their leaders proudly while outriders accompanied the main coach. One many-caped exquisite, controlling his showy steed with some difficulty, rode ahead of the others, unwilling to pass the time riding inside the crowded conveyance.

"I do so admire your carriage, my lord," Lucy, looking quite ravishing in her peacock-blue ermine-trimmed cloak, told her host — who was just then sulking in his corner of the seat opposite. "It is ever so much more comfortable than the public coach."

"You speak from experience?" the earl asked, already knowing the answer — for was there anything this Gladwin chit had not done on a dare or for a lark?

Lucy grinned in remembrance. "Indeed, yes. I was outrunning my governess at the time, you see. Papa had utterly deserted me for Newmarket and I was determined to follow."

"Indeed," Thorpe repeated repressively. "And did you, I sincerely hope, learn anything from the experience?"

Her blue eyes fairly dancing in her head, Lucy answered promptly, "Oh yes, my lord. I learned never, *never* to sit beside a fat person!"

"That isn't funny," the soberly dressed young man seated beside Lord Thorpe responded dampeningly. "You could have been robbed, or kidnapped, or worse."

"Worse, Mr. Rutherford?" Lucy said tauntingly. "You mean I could have been *ravished*, for instance?" She watched with some amusement as a deep flush appeared in Mr. Parker Rutherford's sallow cheeks. "Why, Mr. Rutherford, I do believe you have a dirty mind."

"Leave off, brat," Thorpe muttered desultorily. "Much as it pains me to say it, my cousin Parker is not up to your weight. Now stop trying to shock us all with your exploits and your wayward tongue or I shall ship you back to ride with your aunt."

Lucy squirmed uncomfortably in her seat. "I was only twelve at the time," she remarked sulkily, by way of excuse.

"And are still acting it a decade later," the earl observed tightly, his light gray eyes warning her to hold her tongue.

The occupants of the coach lapsed into silence then, each thinking his own thoughts, and Lucy was free to give Parker Rutherford a further inspection than the quick, dismissing survey she had given him upon first entering the coach in Portman Square. No more than a year or two older than Dexter, he had all the starch of a Cambridge dean, and only half the personality. Dex had told her earlier that he considered his distant cousin to be a dull dog, too prosy by half, and Lucy had no reason to doubt that assessment.

Look at him sitting there, she thought to herself — acting like he's been appointed my chaperon or something. It's not as if I'm unescorted, even if Aunt Rachel is riding in our own coach with Deirdre.

Deirdre. Lucy chuckled a bit to herself as she remembered what her maid — actually shared between her and her aunt — had said when that volatile Irish lass had first spied out Dexter on his hot-blooded stallion earlier that morning. "He'll come to a stick end, that one," Deirdre had commented, giving her carroty curls a flip.

"Dexter?" Lucy had questioned, looking

at the man and seeing a smaller, paler, but still attractive replica of her beloved Julian. "I think he's very handsome."

"Hummph," the maid had sniffed. "Handsome is as handsome does, I say, and that one looks prime for trouble."

Lucy, who had great faith in Deirdre's "feelings," now wondered if her maid could be right. Although, as his immediate heir, Dexter was a prime suspect in any plot to discredit and imprison the earl, Lucy found it hard to believe Dexter capable of such deceit. Nevertheless, he would have to be watched, and she must be careful not to confide overmuch in him.

That left Parker, whom Dexter did not dislike for any reason more reasonable than the fact that the man was a dead bore. Lucy already knew from Lord Thorpe that he felt his cousin to be an exemplary employee: loyal, honest, endlessly supportive, and uncomplaining. Lucy, who was used to complete love and loyalty from all her servants, who were also her friends, could see no reason for applause in that statement. Of course the man was loyal — Lord Thorpe was his cousin, wasn't he?

Two suspects. Two, because — other than to think that Lord Thorpe had incriminated himself — there were only two people even in the running for the dubious honor of being Julian Rutherford's adversary. Well, she thought resignedly, this line of thought will just have to wait until we get to Hillcrest and can examine any clues or evidence that may be waiting for us there. It is pointless to waste time looking for a bogeyman masquerading as either a witless heir or a lackluster personal secretary.

It was just that it was so important that she be able to help Lord Thorpe — and the good Lord knew the man needed help. Just look at him, she told herself, sitting over there like a child whose candy has been taken away. Power and position have been his all, and he does not know how to behave now that he has been brought down to the level of his fellow mortals. How dare he insinuate that I behave like a child — why, I wouldn't be surprised to see him putting his thumb in his mouth, just like a disappointed toddler. If Lady Cynthia could see him now she'd jilt him all over again.

"Lord Thorpe," she said, breaking the silence, "you mustn't look so downpin. Anyone would think you don't believe we will soon have this whole scheme exposed and your good name restored."

His lordship's upper lip curled into a sneer. "Why, Miss Gladwin, whatever do you mean? Do you really think I have no confidence in your ability to sleuth out the person or persons who have perpetrated this malicious bit of gossip? Oh, Miss Faint Heart, how could you imagine any such thing?"

"There's no reason to be nasty," Lucy said, bristling.

"Certainly not!" Thorpe agreed. "My good name has been dragged through the mire; I am, according to your theory, about to be clapped in irons and tried for murder; my mother — once she gets wind of this — shall probably disown me; and my only supporters comprise an overly imaginative minx and my brainless twit of a cousin. Why ever should I be nasty?"

"I am prepared to support you with all the fiber of my being," Parker Rutherford said earnestly, if a bit stuffily.

Julian looked at his cousin for a long moment before replying, "You have a most charming way of expressing yourself, Parker. It nearly unmans me to hear of such loyalty. Of course, the fact that you should be out of a job if I were to swing on the gibbet does not enter into your decision even a little bit, does it?"

"Lord Thorpe!" Lucy cautioned, thinking it unnecessarily brutal to say such a thing aloud — even though she privately agreed with him.

"What? Have I said something that is not true?" he returned, feigning ignorance. "After all, I can't see our friend Dexter retaining my secretary, can you? I rather think Parker has little choice but to be loyal."

Parker broke in before Lucy could say anything else in his defense. "Please do not concern yourself on my account, Miss Gladwin. Lord Thorpe is quite right. I do rely on him for my daily bread. But that is not my only reason for believing in his innocence. If you'll recall, my lord," he said, turning to face his employer, "I was with you at Hillcrest this past winter season. I know you were not involved with any female while we were there."

"Ah, that is more like it, Parker," his lordship said with maddening calm. "Blind loyalty would have been nice, but I find it easier to believe deductive reasoning. I was not openly involved with this Anscom woman while at Hillcrest; ergo, I am blameless in her death. Tell me, my loyal secretary — did you really think that if I were so desperate for a bit of dalliance that

I would go about seducing some poor impoverished gentlewoman, I should *advertise* that fact? Disabuse yourself of the notion that you know my every movement."

"And he said *I* was digging his grave for him," Lucy muttered under her breath, watching the questioning look steal into Parker's watery blue eyes. More loudly she trilled, "Oh, look! I believe we could stop for some refreshments? I vow I'm famished!"

Just then, as if Lucy had conjured him up to aid her in her determination to find another topic of conversation, Dexter rode up to the coach window and called, "My belly thinks m'throat's been cut, coz. What say we stop for a bird and a bottle?"

Lucy closeted herself with her aunt and maid during the time they stopped for luncheon at a small country inn, then chose to ride out the rest of that day's leg of the journey with the women. Lord Thorpe needed time to become accustomed to his new situation in life, and she had decided to let him alone a bit to do his adjusting. After all, she wouldn't put it past him to change his mind and send them all back to town at the next posting inn if they gave him any more reason to doubt his decision of allowing them to help clear his name.

"Dexter has decided to ride inside the coach this afternoon, Aunt," she told Rachel as she settled in beside her on the padded seat, "and once that idiot starts in teasing Mr. Rutherford, I would not care to be within earshot of Lord Thorpe's biting tongue. Dex seems to have such a talent for rubbing up his cousin the wrong way."

Just one hour after that statement the entire train drew to a halt to allow the earl to leave the comfort of his well-sprung coach in order to seek a little fresh air — and a bit of peace — atop the mount he had brought along. Before the coachmen restarted the horses, Thorpe rode up to the open window and congratulated Lucy for having the good sense to absent herself from the company of his cousins. "If one of them ends up floating in the village pond, Miss Gladwin, please don't bother trying to defend me. I confess in advance!"

After breaking their journey for the night at an inn Thorpe had frequented in the past — and having been treated most coldly by the innkeeper — they were once more on the road, hoping to reach Hillcrest in time for an early supper. Lucy had exited from the inn in riding dress, having cajoled and pleaded with Dexter until that young man (who was at the moment nursing a sore posterior) agreed to give up the thrill of riding his new stallion in favor of allowing Lucy the pleasure of sitting atop such a splendid animal.

Her sidesaddle having been dutifully produced by Deirdre, who had packed everything except the drawing-room clock, Lucy talked soothingly to Dexter's horse for some minutes before mounting with ease and riding off ahead of the coaches. Lord Thorpe, who knew he must do the right thing and ride beside her, gritted his teeth to better endure the splitting head that was the result of another bout of drowning his sorrows, and followed her.

"Isn't it a beautiful morning, my lord?" Lucy chirped merrily once she had succeeded in slowing her fresh mount down to a more manageable pace.

"I would liefer it were raining," Thorpe said, wishing himself and his pounding head inside his comfortable coach.

Lucy pulled a face at him, blighting him with her youth and beauty. "Oh, don't be such a sourpuss," she prodded, unwilling to succumb to his poor mood. After all, she was young, she was in love, and she had finally succeeded in getting the earl off all to herself.

"I am *never* a sourpuss," Thorpe contradicted, raising his eyebrows at her. "I would not stoop so low. I am merely above such transports as waxing poetic merely because our thin English sun has condescended to shine. Besides, it will probably cloud over soon."

"Most assuredly, my lord," Lucy concurred, tongue in cheek. "It may even snow."

"Don't be flippant," he warned, refusing to be shifted from his determined bad mood. "Do you know that our host of last evening demanded to be paid before he would show us our rooms? I have been favoring his establishment these twenty years past, and the man had the *effrontery* to demand his payment in advance! If your aunt had not been so weary I should have pushed on to another inn. How dare he — *how dare he* — treat a Rutherford that way!"

Lucy looked at her companion, easily reading the pain and confusion that warred so with his anger. "You should have given the idiot a good bash in the noggin. Aunt Rachel and I would have understood."

"Oh, and is that your answer then? To go

around bashing noggins every time I am slighted because of this dratted gossip? Considering that it would seem that everyone from the Regent to the rat catcher has heard of my supposed disgrace, I do believe defending my honor could become a full-time occupation."

"Of course I'm not saying that," Lucy said fiercely. "Not that delivering at last one good smash to somebody's bulbous nose wouldn't do you a world of good, for I'm sure it would. No, what we need to do is what we have set out to do — discover who has launched this dastardly plot and clear your good name."

"If wishes were horses, beggars might ride," the earl said acidly. "The closer we get to Hillcrest — not to mention the more I am forced into close company with my bloodless secretary and bacon-brained heir — the more I despair of ever being able to show my face in town again. And when I look at my remaining ally — a silly chit who can delight in a bit of sun when the world is crumbling down atop my head — I begin to know the true meaning of the word 'despair.' Oh God, my head hurts," he ended self-pityingly, lowering his chin onto his chest.

Of course Lord Thorpe did not mention

the defection of his fiancée among the trials just now besetting him, but Lucy knew his poor heart must be near to breaking over losing his fair Lady Cynthia. Well, she thought, prodding her horse into a canter, that was one thing she could do something about! Just as she had always felt Lord Thorpe had been resisting his attraction to her, she likewise believed that he was never as committed to Lady Cynthia as the world believed him to be. Once she, Lucy, had succeeded in insinuating herself into the earl's heart, banishing forever the insipid, fickle Lady Cynthia, she would have come a long way toward bringing the man back to his former mental strength.

For she did not like to see him brought so low. It was one thing to picture herself as his savior, but it was another to feel that, to triumph in her mission, she would have to keep taking two steps forward and then going back to drag him along with her for one. Yes, she had seen bouts of righteous anger light his features and stir him into some semblance of action, but these moments were still too few and far apart. He was somehow going to have to be made to take a more active part in his own defense.

"Here," she said, drawing her mount up

beside his and handing him her lace-trimmed handkerchief. "As long as you're going to turn into a watering pot on me, you might as well have something with which to wipe your tears away. Really, Julian," she said, daringly addressing him by name, "anyone would think your back-bone has turned to jelly."

His blond head snapped erect and cold shards of gray ice glittered in his narrowed eyes. "You go too far, brat," he hissed menacingly. "But then, what else can I expect from someone who has such a long history of impertinence?"

"What else indeed, my lord?" Lucy answered artlessly. "But at least no one could accuse me of being fainthearted, daring to bait the dangerous Lord Thorpe so openly."

Julian looked at her for a long time, thankfully not able to see past her impish expression and into her fluttering heart, then finally shook his head. "This is a serious business, brat," he tried to warn most severely, although his twitching lips betrayed him more than a little.

"It most certainly is, Julian," Lucy agreed, winking. "But then, I find being serious such a terrible bore — don't you?"

The earl cocked his head to one side as if

to consider her question. As he looked about him, noticing the wildflowers that grew along the edges of the road and hearing the birds that were singing overhead, his slight smile widened and eventually spread to crinkle the skin beside his eyes. Reaching out his hand, he lifted Lucy's gloved fingers and placed a light kiss on her bare wrist. "Far be it from me to bore a lady, Miss Gladwin." Releasing her hand, he waved his arm, indicating the scenery. "Isn't it a beautiful morning, Lucy?" he asked, borrowing her words.

Blinking rapidly to keep her tears at bay, Lucy responded breathlessly, "Oh, yes indeed, Julian. It is a most beautiful, *beautiful* morning!"

The sun was high in the sky when the two riders, now very much in harmony with one another, crested a hill to look down into a small valley where a traveling circus and menagerie had set up its brightly colored tents.

"Oh, look, Julian!" Lucy cried, clearly delighted. "Please say we can stop there for awhile. We can have a picnic under the trees."

Julian looked at his companion, seeing her childish excitement, and knew he could only be considered the meanest of men if he denied her this little treat. "I guess it would be easier than having to suffer the cold shoulder from some other bumpkin innkeeper," he temporized, turning his horse to inform his coachman of their change in plans. "Don't ride off without me, however, as one never knows what sort of low-life frequents places such as this."

"Snob!" Lucy called after him playfully, urging her mount forward. "I'll meet you under the big trees beside the first wagon."

By the time Thorpe had assisted Rachel to the ground, and the rest of his small party had stretched a bit to alleviate the stiffness felt after four hours of riding in the coaches, he had lost Lucy's small figure in the crush of people standing around a rather rickety-looking cage containing an ancient, moth-eaten lion.

"I told her she shouldn't go on without me," he complained to Rachel, standing on tiptoe to try to spy out his errant charge.

"A word of advice, my lord," Rachel said, unperturbed. "*Never* say 'cannot' to my niece. Besides serving to encourage her to mutiny, it is, I have found, a sad waste of breath. Never mind me now, Deirdre will stand me company. Just go and find

Lucy before she decides to try her hand at bareback riding or some such ridiculousness. I spied out a pieman and will content myself with feeding my face while you young ones play."

As Rachel was only about a dozen years his senior, Julian was surprised to be dismissed as a contemporary of Lucy's, but he was not about to debate his maturity with the woman. He hadn't needed her warnings to know that the younger Miss Gladwin, once set loose in a place such as this, was liable to get up to all sorts of mischief.

"Yes, go ahead, coz," Dexter seconded, running his eyes appreciatively over Deidre's slender form. "I'll do the pretty here."

"Well, I never did!" Deirdre gasped, blushing to the roots of her fiery red hair. "Away with you now, sir. It's a good girl I am, don't you know."

"And just how good would that be, hmm?" Dex said silkily, taking the maid's arm and leading her toward the pieman's table. "Not *too* good, I hope? No —" he smiled, seeing Deirdre's saucy smile "— I didn't think so."

That left Parker Rutherford still engaged in brushing down his drab brown suit, to partner Rachel, who stood placidly waiting for him to notice her. Her short acquaintance with the man had not left any lasting impression other than that of an offhand comment to Lucy that the man "seemed rather Methodist in his manners," but she was willing to spend an hour in his company if it would mean Lucy could continue her interlude with Lord Thorpe undisturbed.

"Mr. Rutherford!" Rachel prompted now, holding out her arm to the secretary. "Isn't your mouth fairly watering for one of those lovely pies over there?"

Parker looked over at the pieman, seeing the flies that seemed to hang in a cloud above the man's head. "I don't believe my constitution allows such indulgence, madam," he said, shuddering dramatically. "But if you insist . . ."

Rachel smiled sweetly and slipped her hand around his elbow. "Ah, Mr. Rutherford. But I *do* insist."

"Then that's all settled," the earl said quickly, bowing slightly before turning on his heel and bounding off to the spot where he had last seen Lucy. "Lord Thorpe cavorting at a circus," he muttered under his breath. "The mind boggles!"

CHAPTER SIX

"Did you know that one of these traveling circus lions broke loose not too long ago?" Lord Thorpe asked, whispering into Lucy's ear as he walked up behind her.

Lucy, who had somehow pushed her way to the front of the crowd that was busy either pulling faces or poking sticks at the woebegone king of the jungle, turned to him eagerly. "Really? What happened?"

Thorpe shrugged negligently. "I heard the thing ate up one of the guards on the Exeter coach. It could all be a hum, though."

"Indeed," Lucy agreed, eyeing the caged animal once more. "Unless, of course, the lion *gummed* the man to death. But come away with me now," she pleaded, grinning up at him, "for that lad over there told me this circus also sports a rhinoceros and a pair of alligators. I had half-hoped for a unicorn, but they lost theirs last month — to colic, I believe the lad said."

"Either that or a lack of ready virgins with laps for resting his head," Julian suggested, feeling Lucy's hand slip into his and deciding that he would leave it there. "The rest of our party is sampling some meat pies. Aren't you hungry after our ride?"

Lucy wrinkled her pert little nose. "Piffle! We can always eat later. First I want to see everything that's here. Do you think they have a rope dancer? I'm particularly fond of rope dancers."

Happily or unhappily for Lord Thorpe's stomach, depending on just how well his aristocratic constitution reacted to greasy meat pies, there was a rope dancer. There were also a gigantic fat lady, a dancing bear, a trio of performing dogs, and several peep shows, games of chance, and an every-hour-on-the-hour performance by a daring man who walked the high wire.

Lucy wanted to see them all, and see them she did — with the earl tagging along beside her, supplying her with coins as she needed them and holding her winnings tucked under his arm. It wasn't until they came at last to the faded red-and-green striped tent at the back of the circus that he balked.

"I refuse to lay down good money for a fortune-teller," he declared, shaking his head as Lucy held out her hand for sixpence. "Only fools believe in such non-sense."

"Of course it's nonsense, Julian," Lucy concurred readily. "That doesn't mean it isn't the grandest good fun. Please, Julian? Maybe the old Gypsy woman will tell me a prince is coming to carry me off to his castle. Oh, please, don't be stuffy."

Julian was insulted. Stuffy? How could she call him stuffy? He, who was standing in the middle of a soggy field holding a belled jester on a stick and a stuffed animal that was supposed to be a dog but looked (and smelled) more like a hedgehog. Certainly he didn't believe he deserved her censure — although he might privately think the events of the last few days had unhinged his mind just a trifle, else why would he be here at all?

"All right, you silly child," he relented, handing her the ready. "Go along inside and cross the old crone's palm with gold. But don't say I didn't warn you."

Once Lucy had disappeared beneath the tent flap, Lord Thorpe stood alone in the sunshine, trying not to feel ridiculous as the belled jester doll waved in the breeze from the string tied at the end of its stick. He felt as conspicuous as a harlot in a roomful of holy sisters, and was determined to call a halt to the whole proceedings the minute Lucy returned. A little bit of cutting loose had served him well, but he still did not feel comfortable enough in this new role to indulge in it for any great length of time.

Already the smell of the place, only mildly off-putting at first, was beginning to oppress him, as were the crush of sweating bodies and general air of abandon that prevailed. But at least here nobody snubbed him or questioned his power to pay. Just imagine, he could loosen his cravat, unbutton his coat, or even slouch a bit, without every eye watching and every tongue wagging. Why is it, he wondered idly, absently twirling the stick in his hand, that it is only now that I have relaxed a bit that I mind the strictures and confinements of my accepted way of life?

But he did not have time to ponder this question overlong, as Lucy fairly blasted from the tent, her cheeks as pale as parchment. "I'm ready to leave, my lord," she told him, grabbing his arm at the elbow and fairly dragging him away from the tent. "I believe you mentioned something about some pies?"

But Julian dug in his heels and refused to move. "Hold hard a minute, Miss

Gladwin. Something's amiss here."

"That's very astute of you, my lord," Lucy bit back sharply, "but as I have only myself to blame, I suggest we just push on and join the others. It's just as you said — fortune-tellers are nonsense."

Lucy may have been putting a brave face on things, but Julian could tell she was only holding back the tears with a great deal of effort. Something the fortune-teller had said had hurt her badly, and suddenly the Earl of Thorpe discovered himself to be angry — very angry indeed!

"There's Dexter lazying about over there by himself," he said, pointing at the young exquisite, who was idly watching a dwarf balancing atop a huge ball. "Dexter! Come escort Miss Gladwin back to her aunt," he ordered as that young man skipped over to them. "I will join you shortly."

"But I —" Lucy began, angry with herself for allowing her distress to be so obvious.

"Do not contradict me," the earl ordered starchily, and Dexter, who had heard that tone of voice in the past, pulled Lucy away, leaving his cousin to bend himself nearly in half in order to enter the fortune-teller's tent.

It took a moment or two for his eyes to

adjust to the dimness before he saw the pile of colorful rags that slowly reorganized itself into a small crone of a toothless Gypsy. "What did you say to that young woman who was just in here?" he demanded without preamble.

The Gypsy ran her gaze from Thorpe's head to his toes and then hastily made the sign against the evil eye. "It's *you!*" she accused in her gravelly voice. "The blond god of eternal slumber."

A pained expression crossed his lordship's handsome face. "That's me, all right, old woman. So tell me what you told the young lady or be prepared to suffer the consequences." Julian could have been more tactful, but he had always found the direct approach to be the easiest in the long run.

The old crone had a belated attack of scruples. "It's the young lady's fortune. It be her secret." But then, weighing her ethics against the gold guinea piece the "blond god" had produced, she changed her tune. "I saw you in my crystal ball. Then I saw the young miss asleep — *dead* asleep."

"And from that you deduced . . ." the earl said, feeling much like a Drury Lane prompter.

The Gypsy shrugged inside her rags. "You're going to be the death of that young lady, and so I told her."

"You stupid old bitch!" Thorpe exploded, turning to follow after Lucy and shake some sense into the impressionable chit.

"I could read your palm, m'lord," the Gypsy called after him. "Everyone wants to know his future."

"Not me, you meddling besom. I'm having more than enough trouble with my *present*," he snorted, pushing his way out into the warm sunshine, which did little to ease the chill that had enveloped him while inside the damp tent.

Lucy felt simply wretched. How could she have been so silly as to allow the Gypsy's ridiculous prophecy to upset her so? And even worse, how could she have been so transparent as to allow Lord Thorpe to see her agitation?

Of course she didn't *believe* what the Gypsy had said — only a complete ninny-hammer would swallow such drivel whole. It was just that she had described Lord Thorpe so accurately — right down to his arrogance. Why hadn't she immediately realized that the woman must have seen him as they approached the tent?

But, a niggling little voice taunted, why had the woman chosen such a terrible fortune for her? Gypsies were supposed to say that romance was about to come into the persons's life — not foretell of disaster. Lucy couldn't decide which was worse — being told she was to die, or hearing that her beloved was to be the instrument of her death.

"Want to go back to the coach now, Lucy?" Dexter asked, breaking into her thoughts and making her realize that she had been standing lost in thought, totally ignoring her companion. "I should certainly like to conk out a little while before we arrive at Hillcrest. Didn't sleep a wink last night in that dratted inn. The sheets were damp, you know."

"Deirdre always packs our own linen when we travel," Lucy supplied, lacking anything brighter to say. "Very thorough is our Deirdre. I can't imagine what we'd do without her."

"I know what I'd like to do *with* her," Dexter murmured under his breath, looking across to where Rachel Gladwin and her maid were reclining at their ease upon a blanket spread beneath a handy shade tree. Lucy, lost in her own thoughts, did not hear him, which may have been a good thing for Dexter, who was known far and wide for his indiscriminate amorous advances.

Lord Thorpe, too far away to hear his cousin's words, but certainly close enough to see the leer on Dexter's face, immediately jumped to the conclusion that the younger Rutherford was taking dead aim at Lucy as his next flirt. Tumbling smack on top of this thought was the stunning realization that this possibility did not suit him even a little bit.

Wasn't it bad enough that the girl had embroiled herself in his affairs — opening herself up to the scandal of being associated with such a social outcast as himself — and then been frightened out of her wits by some charlatan fortune-teller who warned that the man she had championed was about to murder her? Adding an amorous cousin set on seduction was piling entirely too much on the child's plate.

There wasn't much he could do about either the fortune-teller or Dexter now, he decided as he joined the two of them and urged them to begin thinking about reentering the coaches for the longish last leg of their journey. But Lucy, who knew she still needed a little time by herself before facing her aunt — who was so tiresomely astute when it came to ferreting out anything Lucy didn't wish to tell her — said that she was curious to see what had caused such a crowd to be gathered in front of a nearby wagon.

Taking off before anyone could gainsay her, Lucy led the way over to the wagon, the two gentlemen lagging behind, sour expressions on their faces. As Dexter was bemoaning the fact that he must linger in this boring spot and Julian was damping down an urge to give the young Romeo a poke in the chops to warn him off his latest prey, it took some time before either of them realized that Lucy was engaged in a deep conversation with a wizened old organ grinder whose monkey had decided to hide himself amid the folds of her riding dress.

Lucy seemed to be listening intently to what the old man had to say, nodding excitedly a time or two, and then looking most sympathetic when the man seemed to be about to burst into tears.

"Come over here," she called to the two gentlemen once the old Gypsy had finished his tale of woe. "It's just the most exciting thing," she declared, smiling at Julian almost as if she hadn't taken a severe shock to her system not ten minutes earlier. "Oh, not that it isn't a sad thing — which to all events it is, for poor Mr. Romano here — but it is exciting nevertheless, for me."

"Perhaps if you could begin at the beginning, Lucille," Lord Thorpe prodded, trying hard not to concentrate on the delightful picture Lucy made when she was enthusiastic about something.

"Oh, of course," she agreed, smiling apologetically. "This is Mr. Romano," she said, indicating the old man, who doffed his cap and bobbed up and down several times. "And this," she continued, pulling on the lead that led to the small brown monkey's red leather collar so that the animal could better be admired by his audience, "*this* is Bartholomew!"

"I make you my compliments," Lord Thorpe intoned solemnly, exaggeratingly bowing to each of them in turn.

"*Yecch!*" Dexter added, never caring very much for such creatures. His opinion of old Gypsy men who smelled curiously like pressed garlic was not much higher.

But Lucy was not to be sidetracked by either his lordship's sarcasm or his cousin's expression of distaste. "Mr. Romano has just told me the most terrible story. It seems he is quite too ill to continue working and must find a new home for Bartholomew."

"There being a war on, they cannot re-tire together to the south of France," Dex whispered to his cousin *sotto voce,* getting himself somewhat back in Julian's good books.

"How much money do you want this time?" Thorpe asked, not very severely. After all, it would be a small price to pay if it served to take Lucy's mind off the for-tune-teller's words.

"Oh no, Julian, that's not it at all," she corrected, leaning down to chuck the little monkey under his hairy chin. "I said that Mr. Romano cannot keep Bartholomew anymore. I had thought to offer him some money, but it wouldn't really do the thing properly at all. It's a new home that the poor animal needs. Mr. Romano says he's never seen Bartholomew take to anyone the way he has to me. He wishes to make me a gift of him. Isn't that above anything marvelous?" she ended, smiling up at Thorpe, her big blue eyes bright with ex-citement.

"Absolutely not!" Dexter decreed em-phatically before his cousin had a chance to open his mouth. "The damned thing probably has fleas."

At Dexter's words, Mr. Romano's lined, weathered face crumpled itself up like a piece of knotted wood and a huge tear squeezed out of the corner of one eye. "Oh, look what you have done, you horrid boy!" Lucy exclaimed, pointing a finger at the old Gypsy. "That is just too bad of you, Julian," she pleaded, rounding on Lord Thorpe, "surely you cannot be so hardhearted? Just think of the pitiable fate of this poor creature if we do not agree to help."

Julian, wondering silently which of the poor creatures she meant, suggested smoothly, "Monkey stew?"

"Oh, fie on you both!" Lucy exclaimed, putting an arm around Mr. Romano's heaving shoulders. "Not only are you refusing to give aid to one of God's creatures, but Mr. Romano here says Bartholomew is very talented. Mr. Romano, have Bartholomew show us one of his tricks."

The old Gypsy may have been too overcome to put his pet through his party tricks, but Bartholomew was not without some little initiative of his own. The little brown monkey, who had been looking up at the people standing about him and measuring them with his brown-bean monkey eyes, made an independent decision. He scampered over to where Dexter stood looking belligerent and bit the man firmly on the shinbone.

"*Ouch!* Get that mangy beast away from me! Lucy, this is all your fault. I'll probably go mad and die — the creature is rabid!"

But Lucy was already cradling the monkey to her protectively, since the astute Bartholomew had, once he released Dexter's leg, immediately clambered up her skirts and clung to her as if his life were in danger — which, looking at Dexter's expression, it quite possibly was.

It was then, after looking at Lucy's angry face, and likewise taking in Dexter's obvious disenchantment with her, that Lord Thorpe decided that adopting Bartholomew might be just the thing to add a little bit of cachet to his small house party.

"Oh, thank you, Julian!" Lucy cried when he gave voice to his opinion. "He won't be any trouble; no trouble at all. I'll keep him with me at all times, and he can entertain us with his little tricks, can't he, Mr. Romano?"

Mr. Romano, already biting down on one of the gold pieces Julian had produced from his purse, vigorously nodded his head in agreement, not bothering to mention that, besides tipping his hat politely at a given signal, Bartholomew's major talent had been taught to him by his last owner, a petty thief who was just now a guest in Newgate prison.

Dexter wasn't the only one to express displeasure over the addition of Bartholomew to their little group. Rachel limited herself to a quiet "tsk, tsk," which Deirdre commented was a mild-enough censure, considering the elder Miss Gladwin wasn't the one who would most probably be assigned the chore of cleaning up after what were bound to be Bartholomew's primitive toilet habits.

"Oh," Dexter drawled artlessly, always happy to stick a needle where it was most likely to prick a sore spot, "I would have thought such *duties* would fall to his lord-ship's secretary. Parker, my good fellow, you're so good at tidying up after things. Surely you will volunteer your expertise?"

The secretary's pale eyes narrowed for a moment, then reassumed their blank expression. "I serve the earl as he requires, Dexter. But the monkey is not his, not that I haven't been sweeping up after one of his lordship's more trying hangers-on for years," he ended, taking no little satisfaction at the sight of his young cousin's suddenly mottled complexion.

"That will be enough," Lord Thorpe put in dangerously as Dexter's mouth opened to retort to Parker's clear insult. "Miss Gladwin, your arm if you please?" he prodded, turning to Rachel, instinctively seeking out the only person he felt he could rely upon to understand that he wished all of them shed of the place immediately.

As Lucy watched Julian and Rachel making their way back to the coaches, laughing and talking most companionably, she felt a niggling stab of jealousy. Rachel was at least fifteen years Julian's senior. Surely he couldn't be looking at her in a romantic way. Could he?

Poking out her tongue at Dexter, she allowed Parker to escort her to her aunt's coach, leaving Deirdre to fend off Dexter's ridiculous spate of flattery as best she could.

Lord Thorpe's coachman, watching the entire scene with the interest of a longtime servant of the family, could only wonder what else could happen. A bloomin' monkey at Hillcrest? Wait till the old lady hears about this one — there'll be the devil to pay, and no mistake!

CHAPTER SEVEN

Dearest Jennie and Kit,

As you can see, Lord Thorpe has franked this letter for me at Hillcrest, not more than twenty miles from Bourne Manor! Before Kit drags out his dueling pistols and sets off to save my reputation, I will explain that Aunt Rachel is here with me, as are Julian's cousins Dexter and Parker.

As I told you in my first, hasty letter, Julian (yes, pets, I call him Julian now — see how we progress!) is neck-deep in scandal, but I won't waste paper on the exact circumstances, because unless you two are still so besotted with each other that you are deaf with love, you cannot help but know How Low He Has Sunk.

Of course it is all a hum — Julian couldn't hurt a fly — but beneath the scandal lies, I am quite sure, a Dastardly Plot to rob Julian of his title by having him Hanged for Murder.

We have been in Derbyshire only a

scant twenty-four hours, but I can tell you, the air in Hillcrest is Most Oppressive. The servants tippytoe around, forever looking over their shoulders as if someone were about to plant a knife between their shoulder blades, and the villagers — according to Dex, who scouted out the locals to look for clues — are positively terrified! I should be too, if I thought Julian's fine management might be replaced by Dex's selfish style of living. Oh no, the locals do not wish evil on Julian — but it is depressing to see that they have no real affection for him. They only are looking out for themselves.

Tomorrow, our second full day here, we are all going to ride out to reconnoiter. Someone must know something they are not telling, and I Shall Not Rest until I have cleared Julian's name. Poor darling, he has put a brave face on it so far (well, he has had one or two lapses, but that is to be expected in such a proud man), and I know he must be torn between needing our help and wishing us all at the other side of the world so that he can give vent to his frustration without fear of any of us seeing.

I shall try to come to see you, for I wish to see Christopher before much more time has passed, but I shall not be leaving Hillcrest until the Mystery Is Solved!

Julian will be Ever So Grateful — don't you think?

Your most devoted,
Lucy

P.S. Julian has allowed me to keep the most adorable monkey we stumbled upon as we toured a traveling circus on our way to Hillcrest. Isn't he a dear?

When Jennie finished reading, she looked over to where her husband sat, smiling in bemusement as he shook his head. "Who's a 'dear' do you think, love — Thorpe or the monkey!"

But Jennie wasn't laughing. "This is serious, Kit. You read the stories in the newspapers. Lucy's reputation will be completely destroyed, if it hasn't been already. We have to get her away from him — today if possible!"

"I don't think Wellington can spare a regiment, kitten, and that's what it would take to prize her loose. Relax, Rachel is with her." Kit could see one of Jennie's attacks of protectiveness coming on, and he wished to avoid it at all costs.

"But Lucy says something about murder," Jennie protested, rereading part of the letter. "Do you think she may be right?"

The Earl of Bourne drew his wife down onto his knees and kissed away the worry lines that creased her pale brow. "Lucy has never got the straight of anything in her life," he stated with gentle conviction. "Besides, like she says, Lord Thorpe is 'such a dear.' Surely she can't be in any danger. Now, give me a kiss, kitten — your wriggling about has quite taken my mind off any other subject."

"What? Here in the morning room where anyone might discover us!" Jennie teased, nibbling his earlobe.

Kit leaned her back so that he could leer good-naturedly into her smiling face. "Did you think Lord Thorpe was the only one capable of stirring up a bit of scandal? Ah, woman, how little you know me."

Lucy's letter slipped from Jennie's lap, to float unnoticed to the floor.

Lucy was totally enthralled by Hillcrest. Expecting an ancient, moldering pile dating from the thirteenth century and added onto willy-nilly over the years until it sprawled inelegantly in all directions, she was mightily surprised to find that the residence was no more than twenty years old and, if not modest in size, comfortably large without being intimidating.

Raleigh, Julian's majordomo, had told her that the old residence, situated a scant mile away on the other side of the park, had succumbed to fire, with only some carefully landscaped stone ruins remaining to mark the spot. The new Hillcrest, built by Julian's father, had been planned to sit closer to the large pond that lay to the left of it, the late earl having thought it prudent to be closer to an ample supply of water if ever fire dared to strike again.

The fire had destroyed more than the ancestral Rutherford home; it had taken generations of badly painted portraits of past earls and their families, as well as nearly every stick of furniture that had been amassed over the years.

This, Lucy reflected happily as she stood in the bright, airy morning room, could only be deemed a blessing, as she had little love of the heavy Tudor pieces, dusty tapestries, and stained suits of armor an ancient domicile would be apt to hold.

The late-Georgian furnishings went well

with the decorative ivory stuccoed walls, and the muted greens, blues, and rose pinks of the upholstery and Aubusson carpets found throughout the public rooms were just the sort she would have chosen if she had been given a hand in the decorating.

Yet there was something, some indefinable something, missing. Nibbling on the tip of one finger, she inspected the room once more, finally realizing what was wrong. This room, just like all the others, were perfect. *Too* perfect. The flowers, standing tall in their vases as if they knew they would be banished posthaste if they dared to droop the teeniest little bit, were arranged just a tad too perfectly. The beautiful furniture looked as if a mathematician had placed each piece precisely, making up visual squares, right angles, and perfect triangles staked out on the floor.

Lucy longed to tilt the rose satin heart-backed chair so that it sat more cozily near the matching sofa, while her fingers itched to gather up the carefully displayed embroidered pillows adorning that same sofa and scatter them about more invitingly. And the flowers — why, all they needed was a bit of —

"Good morning, Lucy," came a voice from the doorway.

"Oh!" she exclaimed, whirling about to see the earl entering the room, his well-formed body clad to perfection in "a-gentleman-at-his-ease-in-the-country" buckskins and hacking jacket. "Julian, you startled me for a moment."

He bowed slightly, a smile touching his lips as he took in her flustered look. "Forgive me, please. Next time I shall have Raleigh announce my arrival with a fanfare of trumpets."

Lucy was taken aback for a moment, but then burst into delighted laughter. "Oh, Julian, how wonderful! You have made a joke."

A shattered look came into his eyes. "Is that so surprising?"

Lucy realized at once and mentally kicked herself for drawing the earl's attention to what she had seen as his gradual "thawing" ever since they left London. "Of course I'm not surprised," she improvised hastily. "You have ever been known for your wit." That the renowned Rutherford wit was reputed to be sarcastic rather than rollicking, she declined to think about just then, quickly changing the subject. "I see you are dressed to ride out. I hope you don't mind, but I've asked Raleigh to arrange for a mount for me as well."

"As to that, Lucy," Julian said, smoothly announcing a conclusion that had been reached only after spending a sleepless night of rare inspection of his own motives, "I have decided that you should not take any active part in this . . . er . . . investigation. If it is all a hum, you will be needlessly exposing yourself to gossip, whereas, if it is indeed as you believe, a plot against my name and life, I cannot find it in myself to expose you to danger. Therefore, I have concluded that yours is to be a minor part — for the most part already played. Escorting you and your aunt to Hillcrest for a house party did make me feel less like I was skulking away from London with my tail between my legs like some guilty cur."

"But you can't mean that!" Lucy implored hastily. "I mean, I guess you do mean it, but you can't have thought . . . I mean, you can't have been thinking clearly . . . I mean . . . Oh, drat it all Julian, don't fob me off like this. Please, I want to help."

Looking down at the hand Lucy had impulsively pressed on his forearm, Julian — with no little effort on his part — moved to gently disengage himself from her imploring grasp. "I mean every word, Lucy," he said in purposely frigid tones, feeling like he had just torn the wings from a beautiful butterfly. "Besides, I fail to see how I should be in need of petticoat protection — or interference. Dexter, damned loose fish that he may be, has volunteered his services. If he doesn't shoot himself in the foot with that gun I saw him playing with last night, I believe we shall manage to muddle through this tolerably well."

Lucy's blue eyes were bright with unshed tears as she searched his face for some hint of softness and found none. He had climbed back within his shell, she knew, her heart sinking, and there seemed to be no reaching him. Well, if he thought she was just going to sit around the house tending to her knitting, or whatever it was women did in the country, he had another thought or two coming! "You'll make a sad hash of it, Julian," she warned him tightly.

"Your assumptions do not interest me, Miss Gladwin," Julian said dismissively, making a show of lifting a bit of lint from his sleeve.

Miss Gladwin! Lucy repeated in her head, grimacing. How low I have sunk! If I didn't adore the man so entirely I'd go over to him and box his ruddy ears! Aloud, she taunted, "You placed considerable credence in my assumptions when your so-

131

called friends cut you adrift in London. You listened to me then."

"I was temporarily overset," he reminded her, refraining from adding that he had also been three-parts drunk. "This is not open for debate in any case. You may stay or go as you choose — I understand your cousin, Lady Bourne, resides close by — but I cannot countenance your direct involvement in my predicament past the point which you are now. It just wouldn't be proper."

"*Proper!* He dares to speak to me of propriety," she informed the flowers, which were her only other audience. "He, who invaded my home not three days past, dirty, unshaven, and the worse for liquor, begging — yes, *groveling* — as he searched for a single kind word. Oh," she intoned heavily, eyeing the earl disdainfully through slitted eyes, "how soon he forgets. Well, let's just see how well he goes on with the villagers using the high-and-mighty Thorpe manner. Go on, Julian, mount your stallion and ride out to have converse with the lowly peasants. See if they will talk to you, you with your oh-so-open, oh-so-easy air of friendliness. But I warn you, Lord Thorpe — guard your back!" she ended dramatically before flouncing out of the room, stopping only long enough to cock the rose heart-backed chair at an angle.

Julian watched her go, admiring her pluck even as he longed to turn her over his knee and give her a good spanking. Why couldn't she see things his way? He knew he had come to his senses too late to undo the damage done her reputation by publicly championing him at the Selbridges' ball, but no one would know she was with him at Hillcrest if he could just unstick her from the place before news of her residence became common knowledge.

He almost wished he had taken her advice and put a notice in the columns that he was giving a small house party and including a list of guests, but as befuddled as his mind had been at the time, he at least had not been paper-skulled enough to follow that particular suggestion.

Why hadn't Rachel Gladwin used more sense? he questioned, ready to blame that poor lady for his lapse. She had seemed a woman of some intelligence. He walked over to the rose heart-backed chair and replaced it to its former position. "Why are you so willing to place the blame everywhere but where it should be — squarely on your own shoulders?" he asked himself aloud, sitting down heavily. "You wanted her here, and you know it."

A small smile stole about the corners of his mouth as he thought back to the hours he and Lucy had spent in happy companionship riding together along the road on their way to Hillcrest. She was a great gun, as Dexter would have termed her, and no mistake. A little wild in her actions, he temporized, remembering Lucy as she cradled Bartholomew to her breast and calmly introduced the monkey to the rest of their little traveling party as if it were something she did every day, but hadn't he always known that about her? Hadn't her very unconventionality been what had always attracted and repelled him in the past? And was it possible, he thought, sitting up suddenly, that it was her very attraction that had so repelled him?

He shook his head to clear it of these unwanted thoughts. He was an engaged man, he told himself, and had been before Lucy had first barreled into his line of vision three years ago and first set his blood to boiling. She had been an impossible female, always about when he was trying so hard to avoid her, always underfoot, flaunting her small but enticing figure, smiling her "come-hither" smile, eating him with her eyes, teasing him with her —

He jerked to his feet as a sudden thought hit him. He *wasn't* an engaged man! He hadn't been since Cynthia, bless her avaricious heart, had dumped him so royally at that same Selbridge ball!

Julian fairly trotted from the morning room, his haste causing his hip to catch on the rose heart-backed chair and nudge it slightly sideways. "Lucy!" he called up the stairway leading to the bedrooms. "Care to ride out with a bloody fool?"

Dexter did not seem to be best pleased to be relegated to the rear of the small riding party, with only a dour-faced groom as his companion, as Lucy and Julian rode side by side, the former exclaiming delightedly over the bits of scenery the latter was taking great pains to point out. "Thought we were ferreting out clues, coz," he called to the earl testily, "not going on a bloody tour of the flora and fauna. Where are we bound, anyway?"

Julian waited until the roadway opened up a bit and then motioned for Dexter to join them. "I had thought we'd ride over to the Anscom farm and have a chat with Miss Anscom's father. I understand he is a widower, and this Susan woman his only offspring."

"Oh, how terrible," Lucy put in, noticing the tightness around Julian's mouth. "You must find the person who preyed on this innocent girl and her poor father and bring him to justice."

"Yes," Julian agreed, comforted by the knowledge that Lucy understood his feelings in the matter. "Once Raleigh informed me of the magnitude of Mr. Anscom's loss, I realized that my problems pale considerably in comparison. Someone must hate me very much, to go to such heartless lengths in order to punish me. Besides being nearly the only female in this area wellborn enough to suit his purpose, Miss Anscom was without motherly influence to guide her away from giving her heart to a man who had not asked for her hand."

"You seem sure there was a man involved," Lucy said, clearly hoping he would enlarge on his theory.

"It only stands to reason, Lucy," Dexter put in airily. "Deuced hard to make babies without 'em."

"Dexter," the earl suggested coldly, "I believe the road narrows just ahead. Please drop back where you belong."

"Put my foot in it, didn't I?" Dexter asked, taking in Lucy's heightened color.

"Why should today be any different?" Julian agreed quietly, wishing his next of kin on the moon of some suitably faraway place.

"He meant no harm," Lucy told him once Dexter had turned his horse and dropped back to wait for the groom.

Julian looked at her piercingly. "Are you suggesting then that he is harmless — for if you are, I agree totally. I would find myself hard pressed to believe Dex capable of the hideous act we are assuming someone has committed."

"Exactly what are we assuming?" she asked, suddenly not so sure of her interpretation of the gossip that had started the entire affair.

Julian adjusted himself in the saddle and explained, "As I see it, we have several theories. One: the whole story is a hum, made up out of whole cloth for scandal's sake by some idiot bent on embarrassing me or, perish the thought, driving Cynthia to breaking our engagement so he can clear the way for himself."

Lucy shook her head. "No, it can't be that — at least the first part of your theory. For Miss Anscom *is* dead." The second part, the one concerning Lady Cynthia, she did not choose to dwell on, as she was sure that subject would cause Julian pain.

"Yes, she certainly is," the earl agreed. "But someone could have used her death for his own purposes — *after* the fact. We have no proof that anyone actually caused her death. After all, anyone could have written those letters."

Lucy considered that theory for a moment, acknowledging that it had some merit, but not willing to believe it. "What are your other ideas? You said you had more."

"I have entertained dozens, my dear, but a few do stand out as being the most feasible. All right, theory two: Miss Anscom, for reasons of her own, decided to take her life, and not wanting her father to know the real reason, named me as the father of her child."

"You mean, she was protecting someone?"

"Precisely."

Lucy looked over at the earl, amused by his formal speech as he wrestled with speaking to her about so distasteful a subject. "Then it is possible that you are to be the scapegoat for some hot-blooded farmer's son? Oh, Julian, how the mighty have toppled."

Thorpe made a face. "I don't pretend to like it, brat, but as it is only a theory, I imagine I shall learn to live with it."

"But you have another theory?" she pursued, feeling like she was forced to draw every word out of him.

"Yes, I do, and it is the one I am regretfully forced to believe is correct. Someone went to a lot of trouble to impersonate me, seduce Miss Anscom, and then desert her once his mission was accomplished."

Two Lord Thorpes? But didn't everyone know who he was, what he looked like? "How could that be possible?" she asked aloud.

Julian shrugged. "Quite easily, I imagine. I do not make a habit out of residing at Hillcrest. I doubt that my face is that well known, especially this far afield."

"Even if that's so, how could the schemer be sure Miss Anscom would commit suicide — or write letters to all the papers before jumping into the pond? No, Julian," she denied, shaking her head, "I don't believe that theory. Unless . . ."

"Unless what?" he asked as Lucy hesitated.

Lucy didn't like what she was thinking. It was so horribly cold-blooded, so very *evil*. "Unless," she told him, her voice barely above a whisper, "Miss Anscom was a party to the whole thing, only to be betrayed in the end by her fellow schemer."

"You mean, she wrote her suicide notes with no plan of killing herself — just stirring up trouble?" Julian asked, trying to understand.

She nodded her head furiously. "She wrote her own suicide note and then her lover drowned her. Oh, what a terrible thing!"

"Oh! What a great piece of nonsense!" Dexter quipped, having ridden up closely behind the pair, who were so engrossed with each other that they hadn't noticed his approach. "Where could you hope to find two such people — one so deplorably evil and another so deplorably stupid? You'll not get me to believe such a scatterbrained tale, and neither would anyone else. Hoo! And they say you're so clever, coz. Well, you'd never prove it by me."

"Well then, Mr. Smartypants, what do you think?" Lucy challenged, trying hard not to stick out her tongue at the infuriating young dandy.

"I don't have a theory. Don't have to, as I see it. I'm a suspect, remember? All I have to do is stick around so that no one can say I haven't done my duty by my cousin and watch the fun. Tell me, coz," he asked, clearly full of himself, "don't it make you feel all warm and cozy inside to know that your blood kin is here, watching over you, so to speak, in your time of trouble, ready to either take bows if you're found innocent or step into your shoes if you're found guilty? I feel rather like Georgie Porgie, ready to pull out a plum."

"You're despicable!" Lucy cried, believing Dexter guilty of heaping yet another load of woe on his cousin's weary head.

"On the contrary, my dear," Julian corrected her, giving his cousin a knowing look, "I find my mind to be greatly relieved. I now know that Dexter definitely isn't guilty — if your theory is the correct one."

"How do you know that?" she asked, totally confused to see a smile touching his lordship's lips.

Julian just shook his head and replied with maddening arrogance: "Because nobody, not even a country miss, could ever be brought to believe that this ridiculous ninny could possibly be the Earl of Thorpe. If I am unknown, I assure you my reputation is not. Dexter would have much better luck impersonating my groom back there. Their intellect is about equal, although I must say the groom is a better horseman."

"I think I've been insulted, stap me if I haven't," Dexter said, chuckling. "Does this mean I'm no longer a suspect, coz?"

"You never were," the earl informed him, to Lucy's chagrin. "Neither you nor Parker ever was. As I've said before — you are Rutherfords, and above such low deceit."

"I think I'm going to be sick," Lucy muttered, realizing that she had a long way to go in convincing Julian that "Rutherford" was not a synonym for "perfect." Prodding her mount with her boot heel, she moved ahead of the cousins, calling back over her shoulder, "I don't know which of you I pity more — as it is so hard to choose between arrogance and idiocy. Come! On to face Farmer Anscom and see if he recognizes either of you."

CHAPTER EIGHT

Following directions Dexter had received from the innkeeper in Alsop-en-le-Dale, the small party drew up their horses at the crest of the third hill to the north of the town and looked down into the small valley where the Anscom farm was situated. Julian eyed the unkempt fields with the distaste only a good land manager could know, while Lucy clucked her tongue at the neglected state of the small manor house and outbuildings.

"I thought you said this Anscom fellow was a gentleman farmer," Dexter said, breaking the small silence. "No wonder the chit grabbed at you, coz. She must have been desperate to improve her lot."

Lucy was becoming very weary of Dexter's frequent allusions to the possibility of Julian's guilt. "She did not 'grab' for anything his lordship offered, you thick dolt, for *he* didn't offer anything."

"Of course he didn't," Dexter assured her hastily. "It's just that it gets so confusing trying to separate Julian from the real criminal. In my mind I know he is innocent; it is only my mouth that confuses the issue."

"Then I suggest, my dear cousin, that you keep your mouth shut," the earl put in before Lucy could let loose with what he was sure was bound to be a scathing lecture. "The last thing I need now is another gravedigger — I've already got one person shoveling away at my reputation quite handily as it is."

Dexter again believed himself to have been insulted. "Far be it from me to cast aspersions, coz," he said huffily, "but have you never thought that if you had taken the time to be a bit more *human* in your dealings, you might not have this lamentable tendency of yours to attract people who wish you harm? I mean, you must have done something . . ."

Lucy winced, realizing that there was a grain of truth hidden somewhere in Dexter's muddled defense. Julian wasn't the easiest person to like, what with his strict code of behavior and somewhat cruel habit of ignoring those he felt beneath him either socially or intellectually. It was possible, even probable, that he had offended more than a few persons either unwittingly or purposely, yet she could not recall ever hearing a single person speak out against him publicly.

She stole a look at the earl, just now sitting stiffly in the saddle, glaring at his cousin, and felt a small shiver climb up her spine. It would take a strong man to stand up to Julian and thus expose himself to the man's rapier tongue as well as the sure censure of his powerful circle of friends. A covert revenge might be the only way open to someone bent on satisfying some real or imagined offense.

"Despite his rather crude way of expressing himself, Dexter may have a point," Lucy said slowly, praying Julian wouldn't take her words the wrong way. "We have never compiled a list of enemies from which to choose possible suspects."

Lucy could feel the chill descending about her shoulders as Thorpe turned his icy gaze on her. "A gentleman doesn't have enemies. He has acquaintances, and if he's fortunate, a few good friends. It is impossible for anyone to wish me ill. I pride myself on being a fair man, an equitable man. The entire notion is ridiculous."

"And he says I'm digging his grave," Dexter muttered under his breath, "when he condemns himself out of his own mouth, unless he wants us to believe this plot was hatched by his 'friends.' " More loudly he said, "What about that fellow you blackballed for having a grandfather in trade, coz? Or the divorcée you snubbed so royally at Almack's? Then there's old Crosley, who left town in disgrace when you refused to sup at his table because you said he smelled of the stable. Oh, yes, and do you remember . . . ?"

Thorpe's expression clouded as Lucy's gaze slid away from his to concentrate on a patch of wildflowers at the edge of the road. It all sounded so petty and priggish when Dexter said it. "Enough!" he commanded, suddenly unwilling to hear more. Was he really as snobbish and unyieldingly arrogant as he sounded, as Lucy's hastily concealed agreement with his cousin made him feel?

His own recent brush with the pain inflicted by society's treatment of those they felt beneath them made him acutely aware of the pain he himself had dealt out from his lofty mountaintop of self-assurance. Telling himself that he hadn't been acting any differently than any of his peers was small comfort to him now. "I begin to wonder," he said at last, "why either of you put up with me."

Dexter was quick to respond, saying

kindly, "Oh, you're not such a bad sort, coz. Just hold yourself a trifle high, that's all. I lay it at your mama's feet, personally, filling your head full of her notion that the Rutherfords are just one step short of divine."

The horses were getting restless, dancing about a bit at this lengthy delay. "Do you think we could continue this soul-searching some other time?" Lucy asked as her mount sidestepped impatiently. "Once we're back at Hillcrest you can examine your conscience and compile a list of your bad habits. Personally, I agree with Dexter, Julian. You're not a bad sort." At Julian's raised eyebrows she added, dimpling prettily, "Why else do you think I've been making a cake of myself over you these three years past?"

Julian watched Lucy as she set her horse off down the hill, a small one-sided smile lighting his previously somber features. "The chit's dotty over you," Dexter told him, giving him a hearty clap on the shoulder. "And to think you might have been saddled with that block Cynthia. When you find your enemy, coz, I suggest you give him a smacking kiss on the cheek!"

As Dexter followed Lucy down the hill,

the earl steadied his mount as the small smile on his face spread into a wide grin. He had been guilty of the sins of pride and social prejudice in the past — rather like that Darcy fellow Lucy had likened him to not so long ago — but perhaps, just perhaps, it wasn't too late for him to change. He certainly had been liking himself better the last few days. With Lucy's help, he thought hopefully, he just might become the Julian Rutherford she believed him capable of being.

It was only as he started on down the hill to the Anscom farm that he remembered that unless he discovered the person behind the plot to ruin him, he might just learn his first lesson in humility the hard way — from behind prison bars.

"Well that was a wasted journey," Dexter said as he lowered himself gingerly into a chair in the drawing room. "Damn me if that nag of mine didn't have a razorback pig for a sire. Leave me out of any more gallivanting about the countryside, coz, unless we do it up behind your team. If man had been meant to ride horses, we would have been born with leather bottoms, I say."

Julian ignored his cousin as he poured

himself a generous drink before the ladies joined them. He didn't know which had left the worst taste in his mouth — the truths about his character Dex and Lucy had brought home to him so clearly or his confrontation with George Anscom. Even with his newfound generosity of spirit, the earl found it impossible to find one thing to praise in the person of Susan Anscom's father. "Wine, Dex?" he asked, hefting the decanter invitingly before pouring himself another portion.

"I'll have a small sherry, if you please," Lucy said, entering the room and taking up the chair Dexter hastened to offer before holding her breath with special care this evening, and knew that the deep rose gown she had chosen would look its best in the complimentary color scheme of the drawing room. "I do hope dinner will be served shortly, as our long ride today has made me quite ravenous."

Thorpe turned to smile at her, a delicate crystal goblet of sherry in his hand, and stopped in his tracks. She had done it again, the wily minx — knocked him off balance with the devastating impact her vibrant good looks tended to have on his traitorous body. Her midnight-dark hair, with its tendency to curl lovingly against

149

her neck, was just untidy enough to invite his fingers to bury themselves in its soft warmth. Her silken white skin, especially the curving expanse visible above her low-cut gown, drew his gaze like a beacon, while his mouth longed to sip at the moist pink pout that she was just then nervously touching with the tip of her tongue. And the rest of his body — ah, the rest of his most traitorous body — was already light-years ahead of his mind in conjuring up the delights it too could discover.

Damn her, he thought automatically, as he had been accustomed to thinking each time Lucy's mere appearance had this effect on him. No gentleman should feel this way about a lady of quality. It was indecent, that's what it was. But then he brought himself up short, remembering that his opinion of what a gentleman should and should not do — or feel — had already been proved faulty. He did not seriously believe that this physical attraction to Lucy was wrong, did he?

It was wrong when he had been an engaged man, surely. But he was now free to court Lucy with a clear conscience. Certainly the girl was not unwilling, he told himself, fighting down the faint feeling that no well-bred young lady should be so frank with her feelings. Where would he be now if Lucy were just another simpering miss? Still standing in the middle of the Selbridges' ballroom like some stuffed owl, he told himself ruefully, that's where.

Lucy watched entranced as Julian's suddenly tense features relaxed and a new warmth crept into his eyes, while Dexter, believing himself to be a man of the world and up to all the rigs, found himself feeling suddenly protective of little Miss Gladwin's virtue. Seeing the assessing look in his cousin's eyes, and knowing his cousin's determination once he had set a course of action, Dexter knew he was going to have a front-row seat for the courting of Lucy. He took a long drink of wine, wondering if he would be shirking his duty if he failed to quickly cast himself in the role of gooseberry.

While Lucy and Julian stared at each other, ridiculous smiles lighting their faces, Parker, who had been busy since their arrival checking on the estate books, entered the drawing room and asked if the earl had met with any success that afternoon.

"That would depend upon your definition of success, Parker, old fellow," Dexter told him glumly, "and whether or not you wish to work under Julian or me. So far, all we seem to be doing is finding more damning evidence. It seems now that our only hope is that we are the only ones to think there is a plot to frame Julian for doing away with Miss Anscom. A mere scandal will blow over in time, but not a charge of murder."

Parker looked at his cousin, his dislike easily read in his eyes. "You cannot ever say anything without trying to make some sort of jest, can you, Dexter? Cousin Julian is in dire need of our assistance right now, so I suggest you desist from these ridiculous suggestions that you are soon to be the next earl. I find it distasteful in the extreme."

"Oh, really?" Dexter shot back savagely. "How does the thought of me bloodying your lip suit you — that is, if I can find one on your fish face?"

For a moment it looked as if the two cousins were about to come to cuffs there and then, but Thorpe stepped between them, warning: "Have you both forgotten there's a lady present?"

"Two, actually," corrected Rachel smoothly as she entered the room. "Good evening, everyone. May I hope for a report of today's findings? Lucy was so busy preening since her return that I dared not disturb her."

"Aunt," Lucy hissed, coloring prettily.

"We can only thank Lucy for allowing us to enjoy the beautiful results," Julian said, turning Lucy's flush of embarrassment to one of joy. "As to our news, Rachel, I'm afraid it is not all that good. George Anscom was not very forthcoming."

Raleigh chose that moment to call them to table, and as they didn't wish to be heard discussing such a delicate subject in front of the servants, it wasn't until the gentlemen rejoined the ladies in the drawing room that the subject was again broached.

"You didn't linger very long over your brandy and cigars," Rachel remarked, looking mostly at Dexter, who was smiling like a child with his mouth full of candy treats.

"I became weary of the exchange of insults between my cousins and called a halt before one of them stabbed the other with the cheese knife," Julian drawled, scarcely hiding his amusement. "Each was outdoing the other with declarations of their loyalty to me while trying to get in swipes of each other at the same time. I'm still trying to decide if I should be flattered or simply put gloves on them and enjoy the spectacle of having them go at each other on the south lawn. What do you think, Rachel?"

While Julian and her aunt laughed companionably, Lucy felt another unfamiliar pang of jealousy directed toward Rachel. This wasn't the first time she had thought the earl and her aunt got along a little too well. Surely she hadn't been mistaken in thinking Thorpe was beginning to see her in a new light — even admiring her a little? Or did he see her as a child, amusing, soft on the eyes, and flattering in her open infatuation with him, but not to be taken seriously? She gnawed on her bottom lip a bit, thinking furiously. How could she make him realize that she was a woman grown — a woman ready to love and be loved?

"Lucy?" her aunt prompted, clearly calling her to attention. "Julian was just telling me that he believes the newspaper report calling Mr. Anscom a gentleman was in error. Why don't you tell him that story your father is so fond of?"

Remembering the slovenly appearance and crude manners of George Anscom, Lucy smiled as she realized that her father would have enjoyed meeting the man — a man who proved his point so well. For Sir Hale had a fine contempt for the so-called "gentleman's code" that was used to separate Englishmen into classes. Lucy believed this contempt to be one of the driving forces behind her father's eccentric behavior — he kept trying the bounds of propriety just to show the extent to which society would accept ridiculousness from someone they had deemed a gentleman.

Seeing that she had everyone's interest, Lucy sat up straight and prefaced her story by explaining gentlemen in general. "As Papa has told me, gentlemen consider themselves a race apart. A gentleman must have the correct attitude of mind, you know, that puts him above the run of ordinary mortals. Indeed, being a gentleman is a full-time occupation."

Julian found himself shifting uncomfortably in his chair. Lucy made what he had been taught all seem so trivial, so unimportant — rather like a gentleman was all trimming, and no substance. He caught himself up short. What had she said that day in London — that he was so worried about his outside that he was not developing his inside?

Realizing that Lucy was still talking, he called himself back to attention. ". . . and so, as just one more way of proving his point, Papa used to carry a clipping from

The Observer that was published in 1806. I believe I have it by heart." She closed her eyes to concentrate for a second, then quoted: "Singular Conviction: A curate of a village near town and one of the overseers of the parish, a gentleman farmer, had a dispute respecting some private business, and the farmer d—d the clergyman's eyes. For this offense he was brought before the magistrates of Marlborough Street, and convicted in the penalty of five shillings. The farmer contended that he was *not* a gentleman, and that he ought pay no more than one shilling. This objection was overruled, as it appeared that he kept sporting dogs and took wine after dinner."

Dexter exploded into laughter. "That's so bloody perfect!" he exclaimed, delighting in the stony expression that had appeared on Parker's thin face. "The man can damn a curate's eyes and still be a gentleman because he slops wine after downing his mutton. Oh, Lucy, you have exposed us in all our ridiculousness. My hat's off to you!"

"One example like that can't disprove the rule," Parker decreed repressively. "Look at Cousin Julian if you wish to see a genuine example of the English gentleman."

A glimmer of rueful amusement entered the earl's gray eyes. "Yes, indeed, people, look at me. I stand before you accused of driving some poor innocent maid into drowning herself, yet because I have the trappings of a gentleman, I remain a member of — what was that you called it, Lucy? — oh yes, a race apart. Well, if George Anscom, using the rules of society, is to be termed a gentleman, then I'd just as soon resign from society."

"Was he really that dreadful?" Rachel asked, reaching for the silver teapot Raleigh had just brought in and placed before her, clearly singling her out as hostess, a designation Lucy did not miss.

"He was slovenly, boorish, totally unfeeling about his daughter's death other than to berate the girl for going off and leaving him without a handy live-in servant, and nervy enough to ask if Julian was there to offer him some sort of monetary settlement to make up for seducing his 'angel,' " Dexter told her disgustedly. "Other than that, he was very helpful."

Rachel concentrated on Dexter's last statement. "In what way? Could he identify Miss Anscom's real lover — if one does exist?" Clearly Rachel had been entertaining theories of her own, and come up with much the same muddle of motives and means as the rest of them.

"He gave us Susan's personal journal," Lucy informed her, blushing as she remembered the passage she had read before Julian pulled the book from her hands. "It seems she recorded every meeting she supposedly had with Julian — and in some detail."

"Oh, my," Rachel breathed.

"Yes, indeed," the earl agreed. "Oh my!"

"Shame the gel didn't send the journal to the papers, coz," Dexter slid in facetiously. "They'd have raised a statue to you and you'd be battling off the females with a stick."

"That's disgusting!" Parker sneered.

"It's all in the way you look at it, coz," Dexter jeered, wiggling his eyebrows suggestively. "It's all in the way you look at it."

"And we all know your perverted way of looking at things," the secretary said waspishly. "You're a disgrace to your name, do you know that?"

Dexter bowed from the waist. "Thank you, Parker. If I have succeeded in offending you, I can feel that my life is not wasted."

"Oh, stop it, both of you," Lucy interrupted, throwing a quelling look at Lord

Thorpe, who was, unbelievably, sitting in his chair doubled up with laughter. "The journal exists, no matter how lurid its contents. And it records everything right down to dates and times — which coincide with the time Julian spent here some months ago."

"How do you know it's genuine?" Rachel asked shrewdly. "Anyone could have written the thing, and then planted it in Miss Anscom's room after the fact."

Julian stood and walked over to lean against the mantelpiece. "That same thought had occurred to me, especially when I read the journal more closely. Either that girl had a fervent imagination or she had some help. Even the Minerva Press would blush to read some of her purple prose."

"Did you read the bit about the tryst you and she had under the moonlight near the spinney?" Dexter asked, leering at his cousin.

"There you go again, Dexter!" Lucy snapped. "Julian never even met the girl. You didn't, did you?" she turned to ask the earl, suddenly remembering the lurid passage she had been reading before he had stripped the journal from her hands.

All traces of humor were stripped from

Julian's handsome face. *"Et tu, Brute?"* he asked, making Lucy feel like she had just kicked an orphan puppy.

"No!" she exploded, shaking her head. "It's just . . . it's just that I was thinking about what I read and, um, I was . . . Dexter Rutherford, stop grinning like an ape. It's not funny!"

Parker looked at Lucy, who was struggling to regain her composure, and at Julian, who surprised him by looking more than a little pleased at the girl's near-admission of jealousy. "I don't understand," he said in obvious confusion.

"You don't have to," Dexter reminded him. "Why don't you go count the silver or something, Parker? I for one won't miss you."

"But . . . but I think I can be of service," Parker protested, looking at his employer. "Miss Gladwin suggested that the journal might be a forgery. Well, I happen to have in my possession one of the letters Miss Anscom sent to the papers."

Suddenly everyone was interested in what Parker had to say. Looking about the room at the people who were eyeing him either incredulously or suspiciously, he went on, "I visited the newspaper office before we left London, realizing that the

160

letter might be construed to be a clue. Shall I go to my room and get it?"

At Julian's nod of assent, Parker bowed and withdrew, leaving Dexter to comment, "He's a rare bird, ain't he? Who would have thought old Parker would be so resourceful? Not that I like him, understand," he went on hurriedly, just in case someone took it into his head to think he was softening a bit toward his prudish cousin.

CHAPTER NINE

It was quiet in the drawing room except for the ticking of the mantel clock, and the candles had burned down low in their holders as Lucy tiptoed into the room to see Julian sitting sprawled in his chair, staring into the cold fireplace.

Two hours had passed since Parker had brought the letter into the room and they had all gathered round to compare the two handwriting samples. There could be no doubt about it — both the documents had been penned by the same hand, an obviously feminine hand. "Right down to the atrocious spelling," Dexter had pointed out sadly.

It could mean everything, or it could mean nothing, depending on who was reviewing the evidence. To Lucy and the rest of the party it just showed that Susan Anscom had indeed been a willing participant in the hoax — right up until the time her co-conspirator had pushed her nose beneath the surface of the pond, as Dexter had so succinctly put it. To a court however — and therein lay the rub — it was just another nail in Lord Thorpe's coffin, for who would believe Miss Anscom could have been so gullible?

Rachel had retired within minutes of their latest discovery, knowing full well that the gentlemen should be left to discuss the matter without the restraints placed on them by having a female within earshot, and had dragged a reluctant Lucy along with her.

Parker, wringing his hands and bemoaning the fact that he had unwittingly strengthened the case against the earl, also retired, leaving Dexter to buck up his cousin's spirits as best he could. This he did in the only way he knew — he poured Julian a generous snifter of brandy and told him to drink up, and then poured him another. And another. And yet another, until, having downed drink for drink just to be sociable, he was forced to retire to his chamber before he disgraced himself by casting up his accounts all over his cousin's carpet.

The clock chimed the hour, halting Lucy in her tracks. "Impossible," she heard Julian say as he sat looking at his watch, his back to her. "My watch couldn't have stopped. My man winds it faithfully before he puts it on me in the morning."

Lucy stifled a giggle. When it came to unbending, Julian had come a long way, but it was obvious he still had a long way to go. She could envision him standing stiffly in his dressing room, allowing "his man" to wind his watch for him and then attach it to his waistcoat. She wondered if he even knew *how* to wind his own time-piece, then dismissed the thought as she heard the earl give out with a long, mournful sigh. Poor man, she commiser-ated, her tender heart wrung. He must be feeling the whole world is closing in on him.

Not stopping to think about what she was about to do, Lucy sped to Julian's side, dropping to the floor at his knees. "Julian, don't despair," she pleaded, looking up at him with her wide blue eyes. "Everything will be all right. I just know it."

Thorpe looked down at her with brandy-clouded eyes and thought he had conjured up an angel. Clad in a white dressing gown from which peeked the neckline of a soft blue nightgown of finest lace-edged silk, the vision before him blurred a bit and then cleared sufficiently to tell him he had not been imagining the whole thing. "Lucy," he breathed, taking the small hand she held out to him. "You shouldn't be here. It's not proper."

"Of course it's not," she answered, smiling impishly. "Would it be any fun otherwise?"

This was wrong, totally, utterly wrong. He should scold her and send her off to her bed posthaste. He really should. The Julian Rutherford of a scant week ago would have done so without a blink — if not without a secret pang or two.

But this wasn't a week ago. This was now, when his fortunes seemed to be at such a low ebb, when his resistance was weak, when his need for comfort was so very, very strong. Not that he would take advantage of the situation — of being alone in the dark with what even his drink-dimmed mind told him was a willing female he had coveted this age — but what real harm could it do to let her stay awhile and talk to him? None, said the brandy — and he decided not to ask any more questions.

Stroking the palm of her hand with his thumb, and sending tingles of ecstasy up her arm if he only knew it, Julian leaned slightly toward her, the better to see her in the dim half-light. "Thank you for believing in me, brat. I cannot tell you how sorely I am in need of hearing you tell me you think me innocent. As I read that journal, even I began to doubt it myself. It seems so complete, so highly credible."

"Too complete, my lord, and too credible," Lucy protested, squeezing his hand. "I have been sitting upstairs thinking this whole thing through. I believe it was a lucky thing that Parker was quick enough to see the importance of that letter. It is another piece of the puzzle. I think we can be assured now that Susan Anscom didn't act alone. Our only task now is to identify her accomplice. Have you given any more thought to a possible enemy?"

Julian sniffed disdainfully. "It would be easier to give you a list of my friends. Dexter was right — I haven't been the nicest person, you know. But I can't believe anyone in my past could have been so insulted by my actions as to hatch such an elaborate scheme. I mean, this man has already killed one person — just to get back at me? I believe we are dealing with a madman."

Lucy nodded her agreement, and the light from the candelabrum behind her set off golden sparkles in her dark curls, duly noted by the earl. "I think so too. Now we must decide whether the man responsible is either rich enough to have bought Miss Anscom's compliance or handsome enough to have wooed her into going along with the charade."

Fighting back his mounting desire as Lucy dropped her chin onto his knee in a purely innocent gesture, Julian ventured, "I would say the latter, Lucy. After all, the girl was with child. God!" he exploded, his anger at the coldheartedness of the crime coming to the fore. "How could anyone be so despicable?"

"Not how, Julian, but *why*. I believe that we have already covered the fact that men are not always what they seem, never as good or upstanding as we would like. It is the reason behind the crime that will lead us to the murderer."

She was right, Thorpe knew. It was ghoulish to be sitting in a lavish drawing room discussing the terrible crime that had been committed, but they had to face the facts squarely. He looked down at Lucy's bent head and realized that she was shivering, either with cold or as a result of their topic of conversation. "Here now, my dear, enough of this," he said, pulling her to her feet as he stood up. "You'll take a chill. It's time you return to your chamber. I promise not to sulk any longer, and we shall all have a fresh start on our problem in the morning." He put his hand at the back of her waist so that he could help her toward the doorway.

"But, Julian," she protested, tilting her head back to look into his face. "I don't think I shall be able to get a wink of sleep. I feel wide-awake."

Thorpe looked down at her, acutely aware that her cheek was scant inches from his chest. "Shall I . . . shall I ring for someone to bring some warmed milk to your chamber?" he asked tightly, damning his heart for pounding so loudly that she was sure to hear it and now he was struggling against his more natural inclinations.

"Do you think warmed milk will help?" Lucy breathed, nervously moistening her lips with her tongue. He was so close, filling her senses with his sight, his smell, the warmth of his hand on her spine.

He brought her round completely so that his hands rested on her shoulders. "I'm sure it would," he whispered, his eyes never leaving her softly parted lips. Without realizing what he was doing, his head lowered, and time stood still as slowly, oh so very slowly, their mouths came together in a light, tentative kiss.

The fireworks at Vauxhall had never

burst as brilliantly against the dark London sky as did the skyrockets now blazing into a rainbow of brilliant colors behind his lordship's tightly closed eyelids. The warm body nestled so closely against his felt softer than his comfortable mattress, but definitely did not inspire him to rest. The taste of her young mouth yielding so sweetly beneath his caused such a thunderbolt of shock to race through his system that he was amazed that he could still keep to his feet.

This was not a cool, antiseptic kiss such as the pecks Cynthia occasionally allowed; nor was it the practiced performance of a woman who earned her living by means of well-orchestrated passion. What he held in his arms was one totally honest, totally giving, totally real woman, and the realization shook him right down to his toes.

Julian's arms tightened about her as he sighed his surrender into her mouth. She had been right all along; he had been concentrating on the outward trappings of life and not paying enough attention to what went on inside his head — inside his rapidly thawing heart. The fleeting thought that he might have lost her if not for the Anscom scandal sent a fresh wave of panic through his veins and his embrace hardened as he drew her slim form against his body as if he would never let her go. He felt whole, he felt alive, he felt *real* — possibly for the first time in his life.

Lucy was lost. Lost in a whole new world of sensation she had only dreamt of before this magic moment in time. She had known Julian was the man for her, been sure of her love for him. But no one had prepared her for the bliss that she felt within the circle of his arms. She was his, completely his, and every feathery-light brush of her fingers against his neck, every soft sound mewling deep inside her throat, every frantic heartbeat fluttering against his broad chest told him of her love. She was his, his for the taking; not totally aware of how much she was offering, but more than eager to learn.

"Really, coz, I never expected this of you," said an amused voice, causing the two lovers to spring apart and stare in horror at Dexter, who was just then leaning against the doorframe, an impish grin on his face. "I expect it of *me* — everyone expects it of me — but I must tell you I can scarce believe the truth my eyes are telling me. Getting a bit randy in the dull country, are we, or have the banns been announced?"

"Dexter!" Both of them spoke at once, one in surprise, the other in anger and exasperation not unmixed with thanks — thanks that he had been stopped before his control snapped completely and he carried Lucy off to his rooms without benefit of clergy.

"That's me, all right, Cousin Dexter. But who have we here — Darby and Joan, Romeo and Juliet? No. Can it be the sweet, innocent Lucy Gladwin and the upstanding Lord Thorpe?" He shook his head. "Couldn't be the earl. He'd never stoop to seducing innocent young girls of quality. Now why, I must ask myself, does that have a ring of familiarity, do you suppose?"

Julian's hands bunched into fists as he took a step toward his cousin. "How dare you compare Lucy to that Anscom woman?" he growled, not giving a tinker's damn that his cousin had likewise once again questioned his innocence. "Name your seconds, you cur!"

It had taken Lucy a few seconds to recover her equilibrium after Julian released her so abruptly, but like a lioness springing into defense of her cub, she rallied to place her small form between the two cousins before irreparable damage was done. "Stop this nonsense at once, do you hear me!" she commanded, holding a hand against each of their chests. "I won't have it!"

Dexter, who had already begun cursing himself for his loose mouth, realizing that his twisted sense of humor had allowed it to take a healthy bite out of the hand that fed it, was more than willing to call it a day. "The girl's right, coz," he interposed hastily, stepping back out of range. "I was just making a joke, honestly. I didn't mean any harm, really I didn't."

"You never mean any harm," the earl bit out, still longing to hit something. "That's no excuse. I want you to apologize to Miss Gladwin and then I want your promise that you'll forget everything you just saw. Do you understand?" he ended in a voice that left little doubt of the consequences if Dexter refused.

His apology made, Dexter could not help but remark on how fetching Lucy looked, bringing everyone's attention to the state of her near-undress, and she colored very prettily before bolting from the room with a hand to her mouth. That this caused another thundering lecture to be brought down on the young man's head did little to erase the smile from his face, considering the fact that his cousin seemed preoccupied with another problem more pressing than Dexter's penchant for the ladies.

"It is imperative that you understand the reason why none of what you saw this evening can be made public knowledge," Julian told him once they were both seated and holding brandy snifters in their hands. "We have already ascertained that there is a man, possibly a madman, trying his level best to destroy me. If he were to discover that Lucy and I are betrothed, he might decide to get at me through her."

"You're betrothed?" Dexter asked, zeroing in on the one fact he thought truly important. "When you break loose, cousin, you certainly don't do it by half-measures, do you? Congratulations. May you have half a dozen babies — half of them boys. I never did hanker to walk in your shoes, you know, just as long as you don't take it into your head to cut off my allowance to buy nappies."

"Will you be serious?" Julian pleaded, trying hard to remain angry with his cousin and, as usual, failing. "I know you're innocent of the plot against me — it is you who seem to have lapses in faith where I'm concerned. Just let me hear that you understand that Lucy is to be kept safely detached from me until we have unmasked the culprit. I can't lose her now."

Dexter agreed, and after toasting the couple's health, asked, "Was that what you were doing when I so rudely interrupted, coz? Sealing the betrothal?"

Julian smiled then, taking years off his features. "Lucy was saying yes, Dexter, but I never did get around to informing her as to the nature of the question." He leaned back in his chair, looking up at the decorative ceiling as if it contained a vision of heaven. "Just think, Dex, my dear cousin, I'm three-and-thirty years of age and yet I've just been born. Amazing, ain't it?"

Lucy closed her chamber door behind her and leaned against it, struggling for breath. He had kissed her! Really kissed her! And then, when that dratted Dexter had shown such poor timing as to interrupt them, he had offered to fight a duel over her! If she were any more full of happiness, she believed she would surely burst.

She wanted to dance! She wanted to go to the window and throw back the sash to sing her joy out into the night. She wanted to wake her aunt and hug her with happiness! She looked up at the ceiling and breathed, "Thank you, God. *Oh, thank you!*"

Just then a sound coming from her bed distracted her and she looked over to see Bartholomew sitting smack in the middle of her turned-down spread. She would hug Bartholomew! She had to hug somebody or she would simply expire on the spot.

"Come here to me, you adorable creature," she crooned, skipping over to the bed. But what she saw spread out around the monkey stopped her. There was her Aunt Rachel's garnet necklace. And beside it lay Parker's penknife, Dexter's snuffbox, Julian's quizzing glass, and other small objects whose owners must be wondering where they had disappeared to so completely. A silver lobster fork, a small silver salt cellar, a scattering of coins, even a small, roundish lump of metal she believed to be a bit of shot for a fowling piece.

"Oh, what have you done, you naughty thing?" she asked, scooping up the necklace.

Bartholomew, who had been sitting there beaming proudly at his new mistress, cocked his head to one side at the condemning tone in her voice, clearly puzzled. Why didn't she praise him, pat his capped head, and tell him what a good boy he was? And his treat — where was the treat he always got for bringing pretty, shiny things? He rolled onto his side and looked up at her imploringly, hoping that at the least she would deign to scratch his hairy belly.

"Why, you think you've done something wonderful, don't you?" Lucy said, the truth of the matter slowly dawning on her. "Mr. Romano told me you did tricks. Why, that horrid old man! He's trained you as a thief. Oh, Bartholomew, you poor baby!" She sat down on the bed and gathered the monkey into her arms, wrapping his long arms around her neck. "Forgive me for scolding you, pet, it isn't your fault."

Bartholomew chattered delightedly in monkey language, nibbling at her ear and causing her to giggle. "But we mustn't let the earl catch wind of your little talent, must we, for I don't think he'll find it in the least amusing."

Talking about the earl led instantly to thinking about the man, and Lucy made short work of gathering Bartholomew's ill-gotten booty into a drawer and crawling into bed in order to spend the next few moments dreaming of the bliss she had discovered in his arms. Then she fell into a deep, untroubled sleep, a small smile remaining on her features for the remainder of the short night.

★ ★ ★

"Will you sit still!" Deirdre snapped, trying without much success to clasp the single strand of pearls around her mistress's neck. "You've been fidgeting around like you've got a burr in your britches all day long. Now, I've put it before me to fix this here necklace, and that's just what I'm goin' to do."

Lucy subsided meekly on the chair placed before her dressing table. "Yes, Deirdre," she said meekly, scarcely hiding her amusement at the sight reflected in the mirror — which depicted the young maid struggling for all her might to focus her eyes on the small gold clasp. "Far be it from me to be the cause of striking you cross-eyed. Dexter Rutherford might stop chasing after you, and it would all be my fault, wouldn't it?"

Deirdre sniffed. "Him! Such a pest of a man. He's like my father said — only a dog, and will go a part of the road with everyone. Don't think he'll be chasing after my heels, for I'm wise to the likes of him. A mouth full of blarney and enough brass to shame a field full of tinkers."

"Then you're not flattered by his attentions?" Lucy asked, watching her maid's reflection closely.

177

"Soft words butter no parsnips, Miss Lucy, and stolen kisses only lead to trouble with the likes of him. I'll not let my head be turned. Not like some I could mention," she ended, finally managing to close the necklace and then standing back to admire her work. "There, all right and tight."

Lucy studied herself in the mirror and liked what she saw. Her hair seemed to curl more becomingly, her eyes to shine more brightly, and her skin seemed to have taken on a new glow. "You're wrong, you know," she said, rising to her feet and dropping a kiss on her maid's rosy cheek. "Julian is nothing like his cousin. We're in love," she sighed breathlessly, earning herself another sniff.

"Show me the notice in the papers — then talk to me of love," Deirdre said saucily, never one to believe anything unless she could see it for herself. "Your aunt will read it to me if I ask her. I might believe it then, but not before."

"I don't know why I put up with you, Deirdre," Lucy sighed wearily, moving to the long mirror to check her hem.

"I put up with you, don't I?" the maid quipped, lowering a gossamer-thin shawl around her mistress's shoulders. Her hands lingered, giving Lucy a quick hug. "I'll keep your secret, Miss Lucy, but you'll have to hide your face away from Miss Rachel if you mean to keep it from her. If that shrewd one catches a hint of what you were about last night, she'll have you packed and on your way to your cousin Jennie before you have time to take a breath, and no mistake. Now, be gone with you, the gong rang for you long since and m'dinner's getting cold in the servants' hall."

"Deirdre," Lucy called back over her shoulder as she stopped at the door bordering on the hallway. "Have I ever told you that I consider you to be my best, my very best friend?"

Her Irish brogue curling around her suddenly shy tongue, Deirdre gave up the fight. "Go to him now, and may God's fresh blessings be about you." She was thrilled for her mistress, happy to see her so happy, but she could not fight the feeling that Lucy's long struggle to win his lordship's heart was not to be judged settled on the strength of one stolen kiss in the moonlight. And there was still the little matter of his being accused of that terrible thing with that local girl.

No, Deirdre wasn't entirely easy in her conscience about keeping this latest development from Rachel Gladwin. All she could do was hope that the woman would see what was so plainly before her eyes and trust that resourceful lady to keep a cool head. And Deirdre did like the earl. He seemed a good sort, even if he was such a mass of grandeur. Miss Lucy loved him, so he couldn't really be a bad man.

So why, she thought, straightening her carroty locks before the mirror, why did she feel as if she had just sent off a goose to dine in the fox's den?

CHAPTER TEN

Keeping Deirdre's warning in mind, Lucy tried her best not to let her eyes linger too long on Lord Thorpe through dinner, so she was very surprised when, after leaving the gentlemen to their port, Rachel took her to task the moment they were alone together in the drawing room.

"You've been avoiding me all day," she began just as they sat down. "I know Julian and Dexter rode out without you to question the villagers and look for clues, but that was no reason for you to spend the entire day mooning in the garden. Not that you rose until noon," she added, reaching for her embroidery hoop.

"I was thinking about Julian's problems," Lucy improvised, knowing that she was being at least halfway honest. She had been thinking about Julian — about the life they would have, the children they would share, the love they would cherish.

Rachel decided she was too weary to play verbal games with her niece. She had known all day that Lucy was avoiding her

181

for some reason, and after seeing Julian's eyes light up like beacons when her niece entered the room before dinner, she knew she had found an answer. "Just what did you do, Lucy, hide in his chamber last night and catch him unawares?"

"I did no such thing!" Lucy cried hotly. "You and Deirdre should form a club, Aunt; one dedicated to believing everything bad about me that could possibly be imagined. Really, if Papa could hear how you think of me, he would be after you with a stick."

Rachel looked at her shrewdly, her hope of shocking Lucy into blurting out the truth having failed, and turned her concentration onto another vexing subject. "Your papa," she said disgustedly. "That's another bone to chew on entirely. I asked for his help in this matter, but did he so much as answer my letter? No, he did not. How he could abandon his only daughter this way is totally beyond my comprehension. Lucy," she ended, sighing, "I think it is time we returned to London. Lord Thorpe has regained his equilibrium. He doesn't need us anymore."

Lucy blanched, and her hands began to shake. Her Aunt Rachel didn't put her foot down often, but when she did she was nearly immovable. "But we can't!" she said, aghast. "Not now, not just as Julian has begun to care!"

"Has he really?" Rachel drawled, and Lucy hopped to her feet indignantly, knowing her aunt had bested her yet again.

"You are wasted bear-leading me, dearest," she told Rachel, pointing a finger at her. "You could spy for Wellington and tie Napoleon up in little knots like those you're making in that frame."

Rachel just smiled. "Sit down, pet," she said placidly. "You know I wouldn't purposely do anything to hurt you. But don't shut me out, please, for I am too old for guessing games. Now, tell me everything, for I could see Julian fairly drooling over you ever since you came down, and I'm dying to know how you finally managed it."

Lucy took pity on the older woman, acknowledging that since she had been such a helpful ally during the past three years of the chase, she deserved to hear all about the glory of the capture. "Not that he has declared himself or anything, you understand," Lucy ended, leaning back against the cushions and sighing happily, "but if he challenged Dexter to a duel I cannot believe he is merely trifling with my affections, can you?"

Rachel closed her eyes, trying to picture Julian Rutherford squaring off to shoot a hole in his cousin, and shook her head. "He must have felt he had been pushed to the limits. Lucy, you are right — we cannot leave now. But do try to keep some distance from his lordship until this madman is found. Julian shall need all his wits about him until then, and from the dreamy-eyed looks he was directing your way earlier, it's clear to see he won't be worth a bent copper if you insist on occupying all his attentions."

A slight noise at the doorway announced the arrival of the three gentlemen. Looking up at the earl as he led the way into the room, Lucy whispered, "Isn't he adorable, Aunt Rachel?" — a description that had the older woman biting her lip as she tried to restrain her mirth.

"Ladies," Julian said, bowing, "I hope we may have some good news for you this evening, Parker, this will be news to you also."

The secretary hastened to a chair and turned his attention to his cousin-employer. "You have discovered a clue?" he asked eagerly.

Dexter eyed his cousin with disdain. "Oh, stop slobbering, Parker. This nauseating show of loyalty is beginning to wear a bit thin. Relax, nobody believes you to be guilty."

"Why not?" Parker asked, clearly affronted. "I'm innocent, of course, but I fail to see why I should be dismissed by the likes of you. And who put you in charge anyway?"

"The nursery brats are at it again," Lucy remarked to her aunt under her breath. "And look at Julian — why, I rather think he enjoys all this squabbling."

"If I might continue?" the earl broke in, walking over to his favorite spot in front of the fireplace. "As you undoubtedly know, Dexter and I rode out today —"

"I would have gone, if only you had asked me," Parker broke in peevishly, thrusting out his thin bottom lip.

"Of course you would have, Mr. Rutherford," Rachel agreed placatingly. "But then, we all know how invaluable you are to us here, don't we?"

"I think I'm going to be sick." Dexter sneered, lifting a glass of port to his lips.

"Dexter!" Julian said icily.

"Yes, coz?"

"Stow it."

Dexter tipped his cousin an imaginary hat. "Your wish is my command, my lord."

"If I believed that, I might be a happier man," the earl observed idly, before getting back to the subject at hand. "As I was saying before that little outburst, Dexter and I rode out today —"

"We took his curricle," his cousin broke in breezily. "I knew I'd never last out the day in the saddle. You should see Julian's new pair. Bang up to the mark, let me tell you. Gray, they are, and —"

"Dexter!"

The young dandy broke off immediately and looked at Rachel. "Yes, ma'am?" he asked meekly, recognizing command when he heard it.

"You will sit down and speak only when you are spoken to. Is that clear?" Rachel ordered imperatively, and then waited until Dexter had meekly complied before smiling up at Thorpe and saying with deceptive compliance, "You may continue, Julian."

Lucy, who had been biting down hard on her knuckles to keep from laughing aloud, looked at Julian and saw that he too was holding in his amusement with great difficulty. It was wonderful to share this light-hearted moment with him, and when he lowered one long eyelid in a wink she nearly expired with happiness, only barely controlling the urge to spring up and run into his arms after seeing the startled look on Parker's pale face. He was such a prude, was Parker, but she wouldn't want to injure his delicate sensibilities, so she contented herself by giving Julian a little wink of her own.

"Something in your eye, Cousin Julian?" Parker asked solicitously, a question so ripe for comment that Dexter, who had great respect for any woman who could sound so very much like his mama, was forced to jump up and dash from the room before he was tempted to comment.

Finally, with Lucy still having recourse to her handkerchief to dab at the tears of laughter in the corners of her eyes, Julian was allowed to continue without interruption. He told them of his foray into the village and how they had spoken to many locals who swore they had seen Susan Anscom abroad late at night, seemingly on her way home from some secret assignation.

"We visited the deserted cottage where these clandestine meetings were believed to have taken place, but could turn up nothing of any moment. But I don't think we've merely reached another dead end. If Miss Anscom was seen, it is possible the murderer was as well. I've let it be known that I will reward handsomely anyone who can give me a description of her companion."

"Oh, that's wonderful news!" Lucy exclaimed, clapping her hands. "But you should try going into the village at night, when the men usually go to the inns to have their drinks. If anyone had seen Miss Anscom and her accomplice together, it would be one of these men, don't you think?"

A visit to a common taproom was not high on the earl's list of favored pastimes, and this was evident in his slight shudder of distaste. "I'm sure the reward will bring someone to us," was his hopeful alternative to rubbing shoulders with a league of bosky farmers on a spree.

Lucy tried to hide her disappointment. Julian was making great strides, but she would have to remember that nothing really lasting happened in a hurry. She would speak to Dexter; surely he wouldn't be all that averse to a night on the town — or village.

Conversation became general once Julian's news had been discussed for a few more minutes, and Rachel was just about to propose a game of whist when Raleigh came into the room, cleared his throat, and announced: "Lord Tristan Rule, m'lord."

"Cousin Tristan!" Lucy squealed, jumping to her feet and running toward the doorway, her arms outflung, and launched herself high into the hearty embrace of the man who strode purposefully into the room. "Oh, Tristan, how very good it is to see you!"

"I don't believe it," Rachel muttered incredulously. "Hale wouldn't do this to me."

Julian watched the scene through narrowed eyes. Tristan Rule, he mused, struggling to remember where he had heard that name before. He looked at the man again, still whirling his Lucy about in a circle like some Viking about to carry off his captive. Baron Tristan Rule, of course! What did they call him? Ruthless Rule — that was it. He was Lucy's cousin? This unnaturally tall, black-haired, black-eyed devil was related to his sweet, warmhearted Lucy? His teeth clenched together tightly. How closely were they related? It had better be damned close, he told himself silently, or Tristan Rule would soon be Lucy's *late* cousin!

Lucy finally scrambled out of Tristan's

embrace, standing back to have a good look at him. It had been over a year, a span of time Tristan had spent doing whatever it was he did for some branch of the government. Lucy had always secretly thought that he was a spy, what with his penchant for black clothing and his noncommittal answers to her many probing questions about his life. "Oh, Tris, it's wonderful to have you here. Did you hear about Jennie's marriage? She lives not more than twenty miles from here. Have you been to visit her? Is that how you knew where to find me? Oh, Tris, do come and sit down. Aunt Rachel is with me — I know she'll wish to say hello."

"Imp," the man named Tristan said in his low, husky voice, "if you will but give me a moment to breathe, I will introduce myself to your host." Walking over to Julian, he extended one hard, tanned hand. "My lord Thorpe," he said formally and with a hint of steel in his voice. "Allow me to introduce myself. I am Tristan Rule, Lucy's cousin. Sir Hale Gladwin has asked me to represent him here and assure him that Lucy is not in any danger. I have made certain inquiries in London, sir, and I have disregarded everything, knowing that Lucy does not place her trust lightly. Please consider me entirely at your service."

"But . . . but I don't know you," Julian stammered, unable to believe that this stranger would trust him when his acquaintances had not.

"You're refusing my help?" Rule asked, arching one finely sculptured black brow.

Julian shook his head and smiled at the younger man. "Sir, I may be many things, but I have never thought myself to be stupid. I accept your help with thanks."

Lucy released a breath she didn't know she had been holding. Going over to link a hand through each of their arms, she smiled at her aunt. "Now I know everything will be just fine. Wasn't Papa resourceful to have thought of Tristan, Aunt Rachel? How glad I am that you took it upon yourself to write to him."

Rachel Gladwin smiled weakly and wished it were humanly possible for a person to deliver a firm kick to her own backside.

Dexter was over the moon with excitement. Tristan Rule! Ruthless Rule! At Hillcrest! Within moments of hearing the news, Dexter had burst into the drawing room, eager to see his idol in the flesh. Everyone knew about the baron, and whispered of his exploits, but seeing him in the flesh — or, he amended eagerly, in his famous black and white that was all he ever wore — was heady stuff indeed. It was said the man had no heart; that if you pinked him, he would not bleed. He was a paid assassin, recruited by the War Office, Dexter had heard, and his single-minded determination was legendary.

To hear that he had come to clear Julian raised his cousin's standing a notch or two in Dexter's eyes. Julian must be innocent if Ruthless Rule had taken his part. And he, Dexter Rutherford, was to have a front-row seat to watch the man in action. Oh, how he hoped there would be swordplay, for his friend Bertie Sandover had said that Rule was wicked with a blade.

Parker was not quite so impressed. To him, Rule looked to be a bit too complete to be believed. His dark good looks were too perfect, his perfectly cut black clothing covered a too-well-put-together body. Parker studied the man for more than half an hour and decided that rumors about the man's achievements had been greatly exaggerated. Besides, no one was ever going to solve the puzzle of who was framing his cousin. The plot had been built too well for any amount of amateur sleuthing to topple it. All that was going on now was that a bunch of strangers were making themselves comfortable in his lordship's house, eating his food, drinking his wine, and generally making nuisances of themselves. And that dratted monkey — why, just today he had been forced to call someone to carry the beast from his room, only to find that it had stolen his stickpin with the small diamond set in its center.

Yet, stranger things had happened. Suppose one of these idiots stumbled onto a real clue? Julian seemed to think they were onto something, and Parker didn't lump the earl into the same pot as he did the others. And then there was Lucy Gladwin. She and Julian had been acting very strangely — almost as if they were in love or something. Parker didn't like that thought any more than he had liked anything that had happened ever since the scandal first broke.

Getting quietly to his feet, Parker quit the drawing room unnoticed. If clues were to be found, perhaps it was time he took a hand in things. It didn't do to appear completely worthless — not at a time like this.

Lucy had arisen to find that another bright sunny day had dawned, and made short work out of dressing to go down to breakfast, hopeful that she would have a moment of private conversation with Lord Thorpe. He had been polite, if a bit distant, the night before, but the wink he had tossed her made her believe he was not regretting their kiss of two nights ago.

The breakfast room was deserted by the time she got there, so that she ate in solitude, but following the direction in which Raleigh's head had jerked slightly when she had asked a footman if he had seen his lordship, she had blown the majordomo a kiss and hotfooted it out to the garden. She ran Thorpe to earth in the rose arbor, sitting on a stone bench staring into the middle distance.

"Lucy!" he breathed happily when he saw her approaching. "How did you know I was sitting here wishing you would appear?" Reaching out his hands to grasp hers, he pulled her down beside him on the bench. "Lucy, I —"

"Julian, I —" she said at the same time, and they both halted, sheepish smiles on their faces.

"I want to apologize for taking advantage of you the other night," he began, only to trail off as Lucy's little face screwed up into a scowl. "What is it, my dear?" he asked as she tried to withdraw her hands from his grip.

"Julian, you're either a fool or a liar," she said feelingly, "and I am not quite sure at the moment which is worse."

Julian looked at her for a long moment, trying to read her expression. Didn't she know he was expected to apologize for what he had done? Lord, he had all but ravished her, and might have if not for Dexter's timely intervention. He would relax his strict code to some extent, but that did not mean he was willing to toss all his ideals over the windmill. "I had no right —" he began, trying to explain.

"Pish, tosh," Lucy said with a toss of her dark curls. "Either you enjoyed it or you didn't, Julian. Rights don't enter into it when a girl clad in only a thin dressing gown throws herself at your feet."

Thorpe's gray eyes blinked once, twice, and then began to twinkle. "You were a shameless little baggage, weren't you?" he teased, running his fingers down her cheek.

"Haven't I always been, where you're concerned?" she answered, unabashed.

How could one man be so lucky? he questioned silently, giving over the last of his doubts as to the rightness of what he felt toward this beautiful young girl. She was outrageous, outspoken, outgoing, and definitely out of the ordinary. And she was, he told himself as the knot in his chest slowly unfolded, leaving him feeling young and free and very much alive, his own true love.

"Marry me," he said urgently, suddenly unable to form anything near the formal proposal he had recited by rote to Cynthia three weeks earlier. "Marry me or I'll sling you over my shoulder and carry you off anyway."

She had dreamed of this moment, agonized over it, prayed for it. Now that it had come, she was amazed that she found herself able to joke about it. "What?" she quipped, moving into his arms. "Julian, think of the scandal!"

"Brat!" he groaned, before crushing her in his strong embrace. "Willful, outrageous, adorable brat. How I love you."

"Take your hands off her!"

Julian and Lucy flew apart from each other as Tristan Rule planted himself firmly in front of them, arms akimbo. Looking up into the man's night-dark eyes, Julian remembered more of what he had heard about this man. He was a hothead, prone to go off on a tangent with single-minded dedication.

"I am here in my uncle's place, sir," Rule pointed out in heavy accents. "If you have some declaration to make — make it. Otherwise, I suggest you name your seconds."

"Oh, cut line, you looby," came the exasperated voice of Rachel Gladwin. "Must you ever be tilting at windmills, Tristan? Lord Thorpe has already asked my permission to wed Lucy."

Lucy looked around her dazedly. It seemed Raleigh's head had been pointing out Julian's direction to all and sundry. Soon there would be so many of them a servant would show up to serve tea. But wait — had she heard what she thought she had? Had Julian really approached Aunt Rachel? "Julian?" Lucy questioned, hoping her aunt had not just said it to soothe Tristan.

"It's true, my love," Thorpe told her, reclaiming her hands. "But we all must agree to keep it silent until the murderer is caught. I dislike the thought of having you as a target."

Cocking her head to one side, Lucy looked up at him and smiled. "But, my lord, you have not even *really* asked me yet — or heard my answer."

"Really?" Julian retorted, his voice a soft

drawl. "I apologize. I thought you had already given your answer the other night." At Lucy's delighted giggle, Thorpe rose and extended his hand to accept Tristan's fervent congratulations. "Forgive my slapdash approach, Lord Rule, if you will. It's just that where Lucy is concerned, I scarce know anymore whether I'm on my head or on my heels."

Tristan looked at his bubbly, clearly-in-love cousin, and nodded his agreement.

Rachel knew that Tristan would have stood there talking, playing the gooseberry in his uncle's stead, until Lucy and Julian began to believe a flight to Gretna to be the only way they would ever get some privacy. Slipping her arm through the baron's, she suggested he accompany her on a tour of the gardens, a suggestion so alien to that young gentleman's inclinations that the resultant look of astonishment that crossed his handsome features had Julian controlling his amusement with some difficulty.

But just as Tristan was about to open his mouth to protest — and earn himself a heartfelt sigh of resignation from his aunt — Raleigh appeared in their midst, a paper-wrapped rock in his hand. "This . . . er . . . came through the parlor window, m'lord."

Julian looked at the rock with foreboding while Tristan, Rachel couldn't help noticing, bristled all over with excitement. And therein lay the difference in the two men — Tristan was still a boy, hot for adventure, while Julian was a man, longing for a more peaceful, hopefully shared, life.

But, being a man and therefore sensible of his responsibilities, Julian did not hesitate to relieve Raleigh of his burden. Untying the scrap of paper from the rock, he tossed the rock into the bushes and unfolded the creased single page. After quickly scanning its contents, he handed the note to Tristan. "Someone's kidnapped Parker. They demand a ransom to get him back."

CHAPTER ELEVEN

Two hours had passed since Raleigh had brought Julian the ransom note, and in that time they had all learned many things.

Dexter, sent to check out Parker's room, had learned that his cousin's bed had not been slept in, and his questioning of a servant uncovered the fact that the night before, the secretary had left Hillcrest alone while the others were still in the drawing room.

Tristan had learned that although he might not appear to be the forceful sort, Julian had assumed command of the situation, and was not to be swayed from his decision to pay the ransom as soon as possible so that no harm would come to Parker.

Lucy had found out, much to her chagrin, that her beloved had absolutely *no* sense of adventure, and she was still smarting a bit after being told, in quite unromantic tones, to sit down and button her lip before she was sent to her room.

Julian, aware of his position of authority,

had nonetheless been forced to acknowledge that, much as he loved his outrageous little Lucy, she did have a tendency to come up with the most harebrained schemes imaginable.

And Rachel, sitting in a corner of the library where they had all closeted themselves to consider their alternatives, had relearned a lesson life had taught her long ago. Given the right set of circumstances, it is possible for anyone to make a complete mull of things.

Dexter, with his glib assessment of Parker as a "bungling jackass," which earned him a blistering lecture from his cousin; Tristan, as usual, immediately going off the deep end and inciting Lucy with his talk of pursuit and punishment; Lucy, whose impulsive "if-ever-I-heard-a-faint-heart!" response to Julian's suggestion that they call in the law; and Julian's exasperated "God give me patience!" had all combined to cause their supposed meeting of the minds to descend rapidly into a near-brawl.

It was, Rachel knew, time she took a hand in the situation, for Julian was just then giving Lucy a very unloving look, which her niece was returning twofold. "If I might interrupt this little comedy with a bit of reality," she broke in, just as Dexter was agreeing with Lucy that they should be out scouring the countryside for clues. "Dexter, I *do* wish you would refrain from inciting her. Julian, what makes you so confident that paying the ransom will ensure Parker's return?"

Dexter snorted. "Who'd want to keep him?" he chortled derisively. "I still fail to see why anybody wanted him in the first place. Dead bore is our Parker, and it's not like he's worth a groat."

Julian silenced his young cousin with a look, then bowed to Rachel. "Answering Dexter's remarks first, I would say that Parker was abducted when he went into the village to talk to the men at the inns. If you recall, we were talking about doing just such a thing ourselves before the baron arrived."

Dexter shook his head. "Impossible. He doesn't have it in him."

"Precisely!" Lucy was quick to agree. "Parker is too timid to go out on his own that way. He must have been grabbed as he was taking the night air before retiring. I'm sure he's being held prisoner in order to get you out in the open, Julian. Why else would the kidnapper demand that you be the one to bring the ransom? It's a trap to shoot at you from ambush, just like I've been trying to tell you. Since the scandal has yet to make anyone realize that you could be charged with murder, the man has become desperate enough to do you in by himself. Oh, please, Julian, listen to Tristan and stop being so all-fired stubborn!"

"If you are quite done?" Julian said coldly. "No matter what the reason, I owe it to Parker to follow my directions to the letter. To do anything less puts him in jeopardy."

Lucy's lips curled and she gritted: "How very noble, my lord. And what of me — am I to be a widow before I am even a wife?"

"You may be spanked before you're put to bed without your supper, if you don't desist from your childish outbursts," the earl informed her, deciding that, love her as he did, it was time she knew just who was in charge. "I'm not so stupid as to set myself up as either a martyr or some madman's target practice. I know enough to be careful."

Dexter sidled over to where Rachel was sitting, smiling happily as she decided that Lucy would be in good hands married to Julian Rutherford. "I say, ma'am," Dexter opined, watching Lucy and Julian as they glared at each other, "I do believe there is a spot of trouble in Paradise."

A commotion at the door brought all their heads around, and a worse-for-wear Parker staggered into the room to drop to his knees dramatically at Thorpe's feet. "I . . . I got away!" he rasped, before crumbling to the floor, breathing heavily.

Pandemonium prevailed for some minutes as Parker was half-carried to a chair and some restorative spirits poured down his throat. He looked as if he had been dealt a mighty thrashing, for his nose was red and it was obvious that he would soon be showing off one blackened eye. Even Dexter, who would have sworn he didn't give a fig about the timid secretary, felt an incredible need to find whoever had done this terrible thing and beat him into a pulp.

Parker's story, spoken as it was around a swollen mouth and a few loose teeth, was much as Julian had imagined it. Feeling he had been of little help so far in clearing the earl's name, Parker had decided to go to the village and ask a few questions of his own. After finding nothing new at the local inn, he had reluctantly headed home, only to be attacked from behind and dragged off to some run-down cottage.

"The cottage where Miss Anscom went

to meet her lover!" Lucy interrupted, feeling that they were getting somewhere at last. "Then the murderer is still in the area. We should be out there right now, hunting the blackguard down before he makes good his escape."

"No," his lordship told her decisively.

Lucy was beside herself. How could he refuse her help like this? Didn't he understand how impossible it was for her to sit back and do nothing at a time like this? "Oh," she exploded, with more emotion than good sense, "if you had any gumption at all you'd do it!"

"Lucille," Julian bit out from between clenched teeth, "I have had all I can stand from you and your maggoty ideas. Please leave us."

Lucy looked from Julian to Tristan to her aunt and then back again to her infuriating beloved. *"Oooohh!"* she erupted, stamping her foot, and then lifted her skirts defiantly and flounced out of the room.

"That's the ticket, coz," Dexter applauded approvingly. "Break her to halter now or she'll lead you a merry chase."

"If I might continue?" Parker whined, looking up from his makeshift bed of pain.

"Sorry, Parker," Dexter apologized,

shaking his head yet again as he took in his cousin's battered appearance. "I have to tell you, though, I never thought you had it in you. Escaped, did you? Now, I would have thought sure you would have bungled it, if I had ever believed you'd try such a thing in the first place. Please go on, I really do want to hear about your adventure."

The secretary made short work of the rest of his tale, relating how he had been carried unconscious to the cottage but awoke before it was full dawn. He had had one foot already out the cottage window when the kidnapper had realized what he was about, and in the ensuing struggle Parker had sustained the injuries that were so apparent to his audience. "But I broke clear at last and stumbled into the trees behind the cottage. I must have run for miles before exhaustion overtook me and I lay down to rest. I would have been back sooner, else. I hope I haven't caused you too much bother."

"No, of course not," Dexter assured him lightly. "Cousin Julian may have lost another fiancée, that's all."

"Fiancée?" Parker questioned, gingerly examining his puffy lower lip. "Miss Gladwin?"

"Well, it ain't me, you fool," Dexter retorted, back in his old form. "Sorry," he added hastily as Julian shot him a warning with his eyes, "it's just that I'm so used to doing it. Parker here has always been such an easy target. Guess I'll have to rethink the thing. Now that he's a hero, you know."

Rachel reentered the room then, dragging Deirdre in tow. "Raleigh has sent for the doctor, but I thought Deirdre could have a look at him for now."

Parker shrank back against the cushions. "I'll wait for the doctor," he said, eyeing the young red-headed woman warily.

"Is that so?" the maid sniffed, insulted. "And didn't you know that a wise woman is better than a foolish doctor, which is all you'd be getting out here in the middle of nowhere. Give over, sir, and let me have a look at you."

There being nothing much more to do, and seeing that Deirdre would be unavailable for pestering for some time, Dexter took himself off to the billiard room and some much-needed practice while Julian and Tristan, who had been very quiet throughout the whole interlude, adjourned to the garden for a council of war.

With everyone occupied elsewhere, it was an easy matter for Lucy, now dressed in her blue riding habit, to sneak off toward the stables.

It was so confusing. Lucy knew Julian loved her — there wasn't a single doubt left in her mind. And she loved him — had been loving him for what seemed like forever. So why had he yelled at her and looked at her as if he wanted nothing more than to turn her over his knee? And why did she feel like grabbing him by the shoulders and shaking him senseless? This was love? How could you love someone and still be so angry with him that you shouted at him?

As her horse ate up the miles between Hillcrest and the cottage, Lucy struggled with the confusion in her mind. It wasn't as if Julian had entered into their relationship believing she was some simpering miss — he'd had three long years to learn about her. As for herself, she thought, shrugging, she knew Julian tended to be a mite stuffy. It was a part of his charm.

She believed that their love was strong enough to surmount these little obstacles. Besides, Julian looked so adorable when he lost his temper. Much as she aimed to please him, she would have to remember to ruffle his feathers once in a while, just to keep things interesting. She smiled and patted the horse's head, wondering if he really would spank her.

The cottage was just ahead, and she dismounted in order to keep her approach as quiet as possible. She was sure the place was unoccupied; no murderer, no matter how mad, would be foolish enough to linger when Parker was bound to have told everyone where he had been hidden. Looking around her carefully, she tiptoed up to a window and peered inside.

The cottage was deserted. Circling around to the front door, which hung by only two of its hinges, she stepped inside and began her inspection. The few sticks of furniture were old and broken, and only a pile of rags in the corner that looked as if someone had been lying on them showed any sign of recent habitation. All in all, it seemed like she had wasted a trip.

So much for solving the puzzle and saving the day, she grimaced, knowing full well the scolding she would receive upon her return to Hillcrest. Between the lecture she was sure to receive from Aunt Rachel and the blistering set-down Julian was bound to serve her, she felt no need to hurry her return, and decided to ride past the pond where Susan Anscom had met her end.

The village lad who agreed to hold her horse for a penny also supplied the information that led her to the exact spot where Miss Anscom's body had been discovered. It was a deceptively peaceful scene, what with the willow trees trailing down into the water and lush green grass running clear to the edge of the pond.

Breaking off a slender willow branch, Lucy sat down near the gently sloping bank and stared out over the water, trying to imagine what it had been like there the night of the drowning. The lad had said the body hadn't been found until the morning. Strange, she questioned, looking around and realizing how close the surrounding cottages were to the pond.

How had the murderer done his despicable deed without someone either seeing or hearing something? Surely the girl hadn't willingly walked into the pond so that the murderer wouldn't be put to too much bother when it came time to hold her head under the surface.

Perhaps she had been murdered somewhere else and her body dumped in the pond. Lucy would have to go back and read the suicide note more closely to see if the pond had been mentioned. No, she thought, shaking her head; the contents of the letter really didn't mean anything. It was written according to the murderer's direction, not on the girl's whim.

Lucy hung her head, feeling totally defeated. She had so counted on helping Julian, on being the one to save him. Using the broken end of the willow branch, she dug idly in the dirt as she cudgeled her brain for a plausible excuse for her absence all afternoon. She could say she had gone off in a huff and simply been hacking about aimlessly — heaven only knew Aunt Rachel would believe that.

If only she could come up with something, some little glimmer of hope that would . . . What was that? The stick she had been stabbing into the soft soil hit on something solid. Probably a stone, she thought, trying to keep down her rising excitement as she scrambled to her knees and began digging in earnest.

With trembling fingers she picked up the large flat bone button — the sort to be found on men's jackets — and held it up in front of her. It was a very distinctive button, with a thin gold design drawn on it, and could only have come from a coat cut in London. She had found their first solid clue, she could feel it in her bones.

Clambering to her feet, she ran back to

where the boy waited with her horse and headed back to Hillcrest. Wouldn't Julian be surprised to hear what she had done! She had solved the case! All they had to do was match the button to the coat it belonged to and they would have their man.

It was only when she was more than halfway to Hillcrest that she realized that there was no way to go about London looking for that one particular coat. It was ludicrous — they had no starting point, no clue as to a likely suspect. Tears of frustration clouded her vision as she rode on, which perhaps accounted for the fact that she did not see the dog that came bounding out onto the roadway and anticipated her frightened mount's reaction.

A scant second later she was lying unconscious in the dirt, the button still clutched in her hand.

"Take a drink of this for me, Lucy," a male voice crooned, supporting her back with his hand as he held a glass to her lips.

She struggled to open her eyes, but could see little in the dusk-darkened room. "Julian?" she ventured, blinking hard to banish the mist that floated in front of her eyes. "Where am I?"

"You're in your bed at Hillcrest. You had

a spill from your horse. Drink this."

She was all right, although her head ached abominably. Julian was with her. She was fine. But she wasn't thirsty. "Don't want any," she slurred, trying to turn her head away.

"You'll sleep better," he urged, pressing the rim to her lips. "It will help your head. It hurts, doesn't it?"

A small smile touched her lips. Dear Julian. He was trying to help her. "Sleep," she said almost eagerly. "Just want to sleep."

"That's right, Lucy," he encouraged, watching her as she tried to drink. "Be careful, you're slopping it onto your night-gown."

"It tastes vile," she protested, trying to squirm from his hold. "Don't want any more. Have to tell you what I found. Sleep later."

"Do as I say," he ordered, his harsh voice setting off a new onslaught of pain in her abused head.

Choking and gasping, she tried not to swallow the brackish-tasting liquid Julian kept forcing into her mouth. "Stop," she spluttered. "Hate you, hate you for this. Don't want to sleep."

After he had satisfied himself that he had

gotten enough of the potion into her, he let her fall back against the pillows. "You'll sleep now," he said almost gently as he left the room. "You'll sleep forever."

An alarm bell went off in Lucy's tortured brain. "Eternal sleep," the old Gypsy had told her. She didn't want to sleep forever. She . . . *Oh God!*

Lucy struggled to sit up, and the room spun around her. She had to get help; Julian was trying to kill her! She opened her mouth to call for Deirdre, but no sound came out. She was so tired; every small movement became a herculean effort.

Poisoned, she decided, and felt her heart pounding painfully in her breast. Julian has poisoned me! Dragging herself over so that her head hung from the side of the bed, she stuck her finger down her throat and tried to empty her stomach. The top of her head was coming off; she had never known such pain. As the retching ended, so did the last of her strength, and she collapsed against the sheets, Julian's name a question on her lips.

Julian was pacing the library like a caged lion. From the moment Lucy's mount had come into the stableyard alone, he had been fighting a rising panic that had nothing to do with the façade of calm he usually presented to the world.

He and Tristan had ridden out immediately, finding Lucy's unconscious body less than a mile from the estate, and Rule had wisely refrained from coming near him as Thorpe lifted Lucy carefully into his arms and gently carried her back to Hillcrest.

The doctor had been and gone, pronouncing her fit enough except for the concussed head, and had advised them to let her sleep until she awakened naturally. Before leaving, he handed Julian the button he had found clenched in Lucy's hand.

Rachel and Deirdre had announced that they would take turns sitting with their patient, banishing Julian over his protests that he be allowed to watch over her while she slept. But as the day slipped slowly away, Lucy had shown no signs of stirring, and Julian was fast running out of patience.

Lucy had looked so pale, so defenseless, lying there in the road like a child's carelessly discarded doll. It wasn't that he didn't believe the doctor, or Rachel, who had just moments ago at the dinner table told him that Lucy would be just fine by morning.

He had to see her for himself. He *would* see her for himself! His mind made up, he left the library and headed for the stairs, overtaking Rachel, who was just about to return to Lucy's room.

"Deirdre went down to her dinner a little while ago," she told the earl. "Tristan detained me with his latest theory — just as bloodthirsty as all his others — or else I would have been with Lucy by now." Cocking her head to one side, she took in his lordship's strained features. "I don't suppose it would hurt anything to let you peek in on her for a moment."

"I am not by nature a violent man, Rachel," Julian returned amicably, "but may I suggest that it might be decidedly hurtful for you if you believed you could keep me away any longer."

"You really do love her, don't you?" she said, her heart reaching out to him.

"Yes, I really do," he admitted solemnly. "So much so that I am sending the both of you away from here as soon as Lucy is fit to travel. I'm still not sure Lucy's fall was an accident."

They had reached Lucy's bedchamber, and the first thing they noticed when Rachel opened the door was the sour smell that was overlaid with another, cloyingly sweet scent. "Laudanum?" Thorpe ventured, sniffing. "And something else?"

Rachel moved to light some candles. "It can't be laudanum," she told him. "The doctor specifically told me not to give her any — not with the injury being to her head." She looked toward the bed, noticing that the covers had been dragged all to one side. "She must be stirring; the blankets are all tossed about. If you'll just give me a moment to tidy her up a bit, you can . . . *Oh, dear Lord, Lucy!*"

Julian was at the bedside like a shot, taking in the sight of the soiled carpet and the unnatural stillness of Lucy's body. "She's not . . . ?"

Rachel put her fingers to her niece's neck. "She's all right," she reassured him, leaning over to stroke the damp curls back from Lucy's forehead. "She must have been sick after Deirdre left."

But Julian couldn't believe it was that simple. Looking about him, he discovered Lucy's tooth glass on the table beside the bed. Picking it up, he sniffed at it. "Laudanum," he said, and his handsome features hardened into a tight mask. "Somebody's given her laudanum. Thank God she didn't keep it down!"

"But why?" Rachel asked, one hand to

her mouth. "The doctor said —"

"Who was there when he told you?" Julian interrupted, already stripping off his coat.

"Why, nearly everyone, I suppose," Rachel told him, trying hard to think. "Except you. You were upstairs here fighting with Deirdre because she wouldn't let you in to see Lucy. Do you honestly think one of us . . . ?" She let her question dangle, swallowing hard. "Of course you do." She gasped as Julian threw back the covers and began unbuttoning Lucy's gown. "What are you doing?"

"Get me a clean nightgown, will you?" he asked, already stripping Lucy to the buff. "Come now, woman, this is no time to go prudish on me. It's going to be a long night as it is."

"But you said Lucy had rid herself of the laudanum."

"I don't know if she got rid of all of it, just some of it. We have to wake her, and keep her awake, until the effects wear off." Julian was having great difficulty in inserting Lucy's seemingly boneless arms into the white lawn nightgown Rachel handed him.

"And what are you about?" Deirdre's squawk of protest fell on deaf ears as

Thorpe brought the gown down over Lucy's hips.

Rachel filled in the maid on what had transpired before that indignant young woman could launch a physical assault on the earl, which it appeared she was fully capable of doing. "It's right he is, ma'am," Deirdre then said, all business. "We have to wake her. Are you going to walk her around a bit, my lord?" she asked Thorpe, springing to help him lift Lucy from the bed.

"I'll walk her to hell and back if I have to," Julian swore fiercely. "And when I'm sure she's all right, I'm going to assemble everyone in this household and kill somebody!"

CHAPTER TWELVE

One of Lucy's arms wrapped around each of their shoulders, Julian and Deirdre half-dragged, half-carried Lucy up and down the length of the room, talking to her loudly and occasionally lightly slapping her cheeks.

It seemed like a lifetime had passed before Lucy started showing signs of coming around, and then it was as if she was reluctant to rejoin the land of the living. "No, Julian, no," she would protest feebly. "Don't want to, don't want to."

But her feet had begun to move on their own, and the ungainly trio was forced into an erratic gait as Lucy alternately lurched ahead and then dragged her toes along on the carpet. "Come on, darling," Julian urged her over and over again. "Do it for me. Please, do it for me."

"The Gypsy saw it," Lucy muttered sorrowfully, a tear running down her cheek. "Oh yes, the Gypsy knew."

Julian jerked to a stop, his eyes widening in his head. Rachel and Deirdre thought Lucy to be rambling, but he knew better.

His blood ran cold as he realized that Lucy had known someone had tried to kill her. She hadn't merely been sick — she had been using her last strength to try to save her life. "The gypsy was wrong, Lucy, do you hear me?" he declared in a loud voice. "Listen to me, dearest. The Gypsy was wrong!"

Her head lifted slowly and she looked at him with unfocused eyes. "No," she whispered, shaking her head in denial. "She saw you. I saw you. Why, Julian? Why did you do it?"

"What's she talking about?" Rachel asked, as she relieved Deirdre and fell into step with Thorpe. "What's this business about a Gypsy?"

Tersely Julian told her about the Gypsy fortune-teller Lucy had visited at the traveling circus they had stopped at on their journey to Hillcrest. "I was angry at the time, but then I forgot all about it. But Lucy must believe it was I who poisoned her."

"Oh, no, Julian, surely you must be mistaken. Lucy could never believe such a thing. She loves you."

"Hate you, Julian. Hate you, hate you, hate you."

"Of course you do, darling," Julian

soothed, although Rachel could hear the agony in his voice. "Just walk for me, Lucy. Come on now, that's a good girl, you can do it."

"She doesn't know what she's saying, Julian," Rachel assured him as she took in the firm set of his jaw.

"I don't want anyone to know what's going on in this room," he suddenly ordered. "As far as the rest of the household is concerned, Lucy is still unconscious due to her fall. Somewhere in this house is the person responsible for this, and I wouldn't want to deny him the joy of believing he has succeeded in his plans. Do I make myself clear, ladies?"

"Ain't Dexter," Deirdre sniffed. "He's a sorry-looking shrimp, but he's harmless. Gormless, almost." Although the Irish maid was too smart to succumb entirely to Dexter's blandishments, she had evidently developed a bit of a soft spot in her heart for the young dandy.

"*Everyone's* a suspect now until I say differently," Thorpe told her harshly, cradling Lucy's head as it lolled helplessly against his shoulder.

"I wouldn't tell Tristan that," Rachel interposed with a bit of a smile. "I do believe he might take exception."

"That only leaves Parker," Julian mused, then shook his head dismissively. "Can't be him. God, the man nearly got himself killed trying to help me. It has to be someone else."

"Yes, but who?" Rachel asked, rubbing her arm once Lucy's weight was gone, Julian having lifted her into his arms and deposited her on his lap as he sat down on the bed.

"Love you, Julian," Lucy whispered, lifting a hand to stroke his cheek. "Always loved you. Why did you do it? It wasn't nice."

His eyes closing on the unspeakable pain he was feeling, Julian answered Rachel's question: "I don't know who yet. But I'll find out. I'll bloody well find out! Now, leave us, please. I believe she's out of the woods."

Deirdre looked to Rachel for guidance and that lady nodded her head. No more harm would come to Lucy that night, not with Julian there to protect her. Motioning to the maid to follow her, Rachel slipped from the room.

Lucy was beginning to come around, and her soft sighs and small squirmings were having a decidedly bracing effect on his lordship's physical condition. "Sit still, love," he warned her softly. "It's been a long night, but I'm not so fatigued that I'm not aware of the thinness of your nightgown. Or forgetful of the treasures I've seen hidden beneath it," he added under his breath.

"Love Julian," Lucy crooned, a silly smile hovering about the corners of her lips. "Lucy loves Julian — *so much!*"

"Yes, darling," he answered, disengaging her arms, which had somehow woven themselves about his neck. "Just let me tuck you in bed now that Deirdre has put fresh linen on for you. Lucy, sweetest," he repeated, as she showed a disinclination to release him, "you have to let me go now."

Lucy pouted, her full lower lip jutting out petulantly. "Don't want to. Lucy loves Julian." She leaned her head back, nearly unbalancing the pair of them. "Does Julian love Lucy?"

"Julian loves Lucy," Thorpe sighed, taking in the bareness of her long, slim throat as she lolled bonelessly in his arms.

"Then give Lucy a kiss," she teased, trying with all her might to pull his face down to her pouting lips.

Julian looked helplessly about the room, half-praying for reinforcements, half-fearing someone would show up and take this willing female off to some safe place, away from his rapidly disintegrating moral judgment. "Lucy, have pity," he begged, just before she shifted her weight one more time, causing the two of them to fall back against the mattress.

Lucy's eyes were still shut tightly, perhaps because of the lingering pain in her head, and her tongue slipped out to moisten her parched lips. "Julian doesn't love Lucy," she intoned sadly, turning her face to one side and giving a deep sigh.

The last remnants of the wall Julian had built around his emotions crumbled into dust as he slid his arms around Lucy's prone body and laid his head on her breast. "Julian loves Lucy more than life itself," he groaned huskily, very aware of just how close he had come to losing her. "I'll always love you."

Lucy's arms lifted up to wrap around his back, cradling him to her, and he turned his head slightly to nuzzle at her throat. This was madness. She had fallen from her horse just that afternoon. She had been drugged — nearly to death. And here he was, like a randy goat, lusting after her body.

But it was more than that. Like humans all through the history of mankind, he was reacting to the fear of loss by wanting nothing more than to celebrate the continuation of life. This was why man was urged to procreate, this was why woman wished above all things to feel a new life growing within her.

Knowing none of this, reasoning very little as to why he was acting this way, Julian succumbed to his heart. Sliding a hand under Lucy's head, he lifted her face to his and allowed nature to take its course.

She was all response, all fire and fluid, giving everything while taking all, and he was totally lost. Her mouth burned beneath his, her body molded to his as if fashioned for just that purpose, her hands branded his face, his neck, his back.

"Lucy, my dearest, darling Lucy," he breathed, his hands shaking as he fumbled with the opening of her gown. "Always and forever, my darling Lucy."

Lucy was floating. Her head, which had been pounding so fiercely just minutes earlier, was now numb to everything but the sensations sent to it from her gloriously alive body. Julian was here; Julian holding her, touching her, kissing her. Julian was her love. Julian was . . .

"Julian," she whispered into the ear she

was just then nibbling. "Why did you hurt me?"

His hands stilled on the third button from the top of her gown. She still thought that he had been the one who had tried to kill her. His blood ran cold, succeeding in immediately cooling his ardor, though not his fierce love of this girl who could still love him, believing him guilty of trying to murder her.

"Lucy," he begged, stroking her head as he willed his words to penetrate the hazy world of sensation Lucy still inhabited, "I didn't do it. I'd never hurt you. I swear to you, with God as my judge, that I would never harm a single hair on your adorable head."

The fact that he had come perilously close to deflowering his "love" while she was in a near-senseless state caused him to grimace as if he were in deepest pain, but he knew he would have to reserve his guilty feelings to be dealt with later. Right now it was imperative that Lucy be brought to understand that he loved her — would never harm her. "Lucy, you must believe me!" he said, shaking her slightly for emphasis. "My God, please!"

But Lucy was at last slipping into a healing, restful sleep. The last thing she did before her tightly closed eyelids relaxed into a more normal expression was to lift her hand to Julian's cheek and sigh. "It's all right, Julian. All right. Still love you."

He caught her hand as it began to slip away and pressed his lips into her palm. Then, realizing that further attempts to rouse her much before midday would be fruitless, he shifted her body to the middle of the bed and drew up the covers.

He stood beside the bed for a long time, watching over her as she slept. It was nearly dawn before he spoke again, so softly that Rachel, who had peeked in to check on her niece, could barely hear his words. "I'll kill the bloody bastard!" he rasped, his hands clenched into tight fists at his sides. "I swear to God I'll kill him!"

The sun was fairly high before Julian stirred from his chair in front of the cold fireplace in his, the master bedchamber. Calling for his man, he took advantage of a refreshing bath and allowed himself to be dressed in the casual country elegance that took all of his valet's efforts to create, and then dismissed the servant.

He had already missed the breakfast buffet and it still lacked two hours to luncheon, although he couldn't have forced a single forkful of food past his firmly compressed lips. His whole mind, his entire being, was concentrating on discovering some way to ferret out the murderer and then slowly, carefully, take the bastard apart bit by satisfying bit.

But how was he to succeed now when to date they had all been failing so miserably? There were no new clues, only a new crime; a crime that cast into the shade the plot to discredit his name. If he had been told a fortnight ago that there was a single thing on the earth that mattered more than his reputation, he would have laughed at the absurdity of anything taking precedence over his pride in his lineage.

But now he had learned, through bitter experience, the folly of his previous values. If he could trade all his good name and blue-blooded ancestors for Lucy's safety, he would do so without a blink. All that mattered to him, all that gave him reason to draw breath, was wrapped up in the slim young girl lying injured and vulnerable in her chamber down the hallway.

He had thought over his options as dawn broke over the countryside, and he had decided, not without regret, that the only person, besides Rachel and Deirdre, that he could trust to stand his ally was Tristan

Rule — not because he was about to accept the man on blind faith, but because he had been out of the country during the time the scandal broke.

Tristan had a reputation for his intelligence, his loyalty to his friends and his country, his dogged determination. That these attributes could, according to what he had learned from Rachel, also lead Rule to pigheadedness, single-minded pursuit of his own peculiar interpretation of justice, and his well-earned nickname of "Ruthless Rule" was not something he had the luxury of refining on at the moment.

Thorpe was just about to ring for a servant, sending him off with the request that Lord Rule join him in his chambers, when a slight scratching at his chamber door caught his attention. Crossing to the door as quietly as possible, he flung it open in order to surprise whoever was eavesdropping outside.

No one was there. He leaned his head out the door to check the hallway, which was empty of servants or guests, and then his attention was brought closer to the ground. Sitting on his haunches at his lordship's feet was a small brown furry creature, a jaunty red cap pushed down over his ears.

"Bartholomew!" Julian chuckled. "What mischief are you up to this time?" Leaning down to scoop the smiling, chattering monkey into his arms, Thorpe stepped back into his chamber and closed the door.

It would have surprised all who might have been witness to Thorpe's warm reception of the monkey — all but the earl's long-suffering valet, that is, who had spent many an hour brushing stubborn monkey hairs from his master's dressing gown — to know that Bartholomew was a frequent guest in his lordship's private chamber.

Bartholomew was loyal to his new mistress, but perhaps because the creature was accustomed to a male master, he had made it a point to seek Thorpe out. Julian, striving with all his might to become a more open, generous sort of soul, had begun his association with Bartholomew as a gesture of his good intentions, and then pursued the acquaintance when the little monkey, who was quite an affectionate monster, slowly wormed his way into the earl's heart.

It followed most naturally that Julian, rather than Lucy, became the recipient of the items gleaned from Bartholomew's latest foraging expeditions. Lucy, who had not told Julian of Bartholomew's little trick for fear the creature would be punished or even expelled from Hillcrest, had only silently rejoiced when the monkey stopped bringing her thimbles, diamond earrings, and golden guineas.

For his part, Julian saw no reason to inform Lucy of her new pet's larcenous tendencies. All in all, for Bartholomew at least, it made for a satisfying resolution. For the rest of the household, it mattered little either way, for Julian had made it a practice to leave anything of value out in the open where its owners could find it, thinking the item had been merely mislaid, and he still could fill a hatbox with the other miscellaneous booty, so that Bartholomew could play with his treasures during his daily visits.

"What have you pilfered today, O bold highwayman?" Thorpe asked the monkey, setting the creature down on his bed. He needed a moment's respite from his troubles, and looking through Bartholomew's latest haul should provide a small diversion.

"Aha! And what is this?" he questioned, holding up a silver paperweight as the delighted monkey rolled over on the bed and awaited his reward, a satisfying scratching of his tight belly. "Pleased with yourself, aren't you, you little imp of mischief?"

Bartholomew bared his teeth in a wide monkey smile and reached into the little leather pouch that hung around his neck to pull out yet another treasure for his master's delectation and admiration.

Julian's smile faded as he took the object from Bartholomew's fingers and held it to the light. "Isn't that interesting," he mused, rubbing the shiny object between his fingertips. Looking down at the monkey, he asked quietly, "Do you know where you got this, Bartholomew?" The monkey tipped his head and looked at his master inquiringly. Didn't he like it?

Realizing his error, Thorpe proceeded to make a very great business out of congratulating Bartholomew for bringing such a wonderful gift. "Can you bring me another one like it?" he asked the monkey, making clasping motions against his chest, as if to say "More, more." Did the monkey understand? Julian asked himself, his heart beginning to pound as he felt he was hovering on the brink of discovering something truly important.

Bartholomew scampered down from the high bed and over to the door, chattering happily as he waited for the earl to let him out into the hallway.

Looking about quickly to see that the corridor was still deserted, Julian headed off in Bartholomew's wake, hoping against hope that the monkey was leading him straight to the man who had nearly succeeded in his attempt to murder Lucy.

Julian was beginning to wish he had kept his own counsel. Not only was he getting a crick in his neck from watching Lord Rule as that man paced back and forth across the library carpet (at twice the pace of any other gentleman, but then Lord Rule seemed to do everything with more intensity than any other gentleman), but listening to the man as he described, in graphic detail, just what he would do with the murderer once he got his hands on him was becoming just the teeniest bit annoying.

"Leave the disposition of the man to me," Julian told Tristan, just as the younger man was in the midst of describing the colors the murderer's face would turn as he, as avenger, wrung the man's scrawny neck.

"Just tell me who he is!" Rule demanded for the hundredth time. "I can tell that you know. If you trust me enough to ask me to guard your back, you can tell me whom to guard it against, damn it all to hell! Why don't you give me his name?"

Thorpe looked at Rule, surprised to see that no fire spewed from his mouth as the young hothead spoke. Shaking his head, Julian thanked his lucky stars that the sight of Rule in a temper had served to bring himself back to reason. He would capture the murderer and see that the man was punished. But vengeance, earlier his only desire, was not the way for a sane man to go. In the end, revenge merely for the sake of the satisfaction he would feel in having the man lying dead at his feet would cut at him as well.

"I'm not going to tell you," he stated firmly now, "because I wish to save you from the gallows. The moment you hear the suspect's name you will go off with murder in your eye — that's as plain to me as is the nose on your face — a nose, by the by, that seems to be breathing smoke at the moment."

"Don't you care that Lucy was nearly killed?" Tristan asked indignantly, looking at Thorpe through dark, narrowed eyes.

The earl jumped to his feet. "That will be enough!" he exclaimed coldly. "I said I have a suspect, a very good suspect. I can't have you going off slaying suspects like you would dragons, until we rid the forest of anyone who seems the least bit suspicious. And," he ended haughtily, "if you ever again question my love and concern for your cousin, sir, you may prepare yourself for the drubbing of your life. Now, are you with me or not?"

Rule ran a hand through his already disordered hair. "My apologies, Thorpe," he offered sincerely, if not humbly.

"Accepted," Julian agreed, and the two men sat down to plan strategy, only to be interrupted by Raleigh as he announced the arrival of Lord and Lady Bourne.

"Jennie, here?" Tristan exclaimed, jumping up so swiftly that he nearly knocked over the chair.

Julian watched, amused, as yet another man looked askance as Tristan Rule, the handsome devil, whirled yet another young, beautiful woman about him as that young woman clung to him in ecstasy. Walking over to Kit Wilde, Julian extended his hand. "Lord Bourne?" he offered silkily. "Perhaps we should join forces and petition the War Office to send him to the front. He does seem to have a most unsettling way with the ladies, doesn't he?"

Kit took the hand Thorpe offered and returned the greeting, not quite sure that this was the same Lord Thorpe he had so thoroughly disliked during his time in London. "The country air seems to agree with you, Thorpe," he remarked, unable at the moment to say anything more sensible.

Julian smiled ruefully. "Being in love with the most beautiful woman in the world agrees with me, Lord Bourne. If your countess is anything like my Lucy, I'm sure we are both changed men."

Jennie, who had been watching her husband and the earl out of the corners of her eyes, dragged Tristan over to meet Kit, saying smugly, "I knew Lucy could do it, dearest. Now we have only Tristan here to settle, and I will be the happiest of women."

Kit drew Jennie into the crook of his arm as he and Tristan shook hands. "Consider yourself warned, my friend," he said jokingly. "My Jennie is happy only when she is settling other people's lives. Oh, the stories I could tell you — but I'll refrain, for fear I should scare you off. Jennie would never forgive me."

"Where's Lucy?" Jennie interrupted, not at all insulted by her husband's words. "We've been quite worried about her, my lord, which is why we have barged in on you so rudely."

Surprisingly, it was Lord Rule who stepped into the breach, explaining that Lucy had taken a slight spill from her horse the day before, and Jennie watched Thorpe closely, hugely gratified to see the concern so clearly written on his face.

For Jennie had received a letter from a friend in London just the day before, which turned out to be the final, convincing argument that had made Kit agree to their visit to Hillcrest. Lady Cynthia's father had announced his daughter's engagement to Lord Seabrook.

It had been Jennie's intention to warn Lucy of this new development before Thorpe could get wind of it through an announcement in the papers, which, fortunately, took so long to reach the country. And yet, she thought, smiling beautifully as Thorpe talked about Lucy with her husband, she now believed that her errand of mercy had been turned into a congratulatory visit.

Rachel Gladwin's entrance into the room confirmed that suspicion, as Jennie quickly cornered her to ask that already answered question: "How fares the campaign?" Her mind no longer troubled, she was ready to hear all the juicy details!

After a pleasant luncheon, a little delayed by the temper tantrum the chef threw after being informed there were to be two more at table, besides the special invalid gruels he had to prepare for Lucy and the tender-mouthed Parker, the men returned to the library to bring Kit up-to-date on events, while the ladies mounted the stairs to check on Lucy's recovery.

With Parker nursing his wounds in his chamber, Dexter, who was smarting a bit at being left out of things, decided to seek out Deirdre and discover whether or not she would like to spend an edifying half-hour in the deserted nursery wing indulging in a little game he had thought up in his idle hours.

All in all, the afternoon passed swiftly, and the growing house party, to an outsider, seemed quite ordinary. It was only as the dinner hour approached, when Lucy would insist on dressing and sitting at the table, that matters were to come to a head.

CHAPTER THIRTEEN

Lucy had awakened, much refreshed by two of the afternoon, immediately remembering the events of the previous night, although those memories came in spurts, not necessarily in order, and served to confuse her not a little bit.

Julian had come into her room and forced her to drink something vile that was meant to poison her. No, she objected, shaking her head (which still ached a bit), Julian had come to her room to save her! She could remember him walking her up and down the room, urging her to wake up and talk to him. And she had awakened, finding herself to be snuggled cozily in his arms, and they had . . . Oh dear! They nearly had, hadn't they! She pressed her hands to her flaming cheeks. She remembered now — she had tried to seduce him!

And not without a good deal of success, she recalled, smiling a bit in spite of herself before her nagging brain recalled for her the ending of that particular scene. She had accused Julian of trying to murder her!

How utterly ridiculous a thought. It couldn't have been Julian. Julian loved her. It had been dark in the room, she told herself, not realizing that it could just as well have been full daylight, for she had kept her eyes tightly closed the whole time, and she couldn't say for sure just who had forced the poison down her throat.

Thank goodness she had remembered the Gypsy's warning — even if the old woman had not quite got the straight of it. A man had tried to murder her — but that man wasn't Julian Rutherford. Lucy lay in bed gnawing on her knuckle, trying with all her might to remember more about her attacker. Yes, it was a man — but who? As to the *why* of the thing, that she would think about later. At the moment, putting a name to the man was paramount in her mind.

Closing her eyes, she tried to recall the feel of the man's body as he had held her, but her memory failed her. Even the Gypsy, with her description of a "blond god of eternal sleep," was of little use. All three Rutherford men were blonds. If only her mind didn't keep straying from the point to concentrate on the memory of Julian's face as it hovered over hers, the feel of his hands as they roved over her body, the scent of his warm breath as he —

"Lucy! You poor darling creature!"

"Jennie! You, here? How marvelous a surprise!" Lucy struggled to sit up in the midst of her tangled bedcovers and was soon wrapped in her cousin's tight embrace.

What followed was a typical meeting between the two, full of teasing banter, shared secrets, and more than a few silly giggles, but at last they sobered, and Lucy brought Jennie up-to-date on what had transpired since her last letter.

". . . and so, thanks to Julian's astute reading of the situation, for it seems to me he acted quite rightly, not to mention my own quick thinking — helped by my remembrance of the murder plot in some novel I read long ago — I am here today, ready to help Julian unmask our murderer. Then," she added, hugging herself happily, "we shall be married. Isn't it just like something out of a storybook?"

Jennie tried to look pleased, but a small frown persisted as she said what she had to say. "I received a letter from London, pet, telling me of Lady Cynthia's betrothal to Lord Seabrook."

Lucy surprised her cousin by clapping her hands in glee. "Oh, it couldn't possibly be any better!" she exclaimed. "It just goes to show that Deirdre's right in her Irish sayings: 'There never was an old slipper but there was an old stocking to match it.' They are a perfect match — a marriage made in their papas' pocketbooks."

"You compare Lady Cynthia to a *shoe?*" Jennie asked, giggling a bit in spite of herself. "Lucy, how naughty!"

Lucy pretended to pout. "Well, she did give Julian the *boot,* didn't she?" she asked facetiously. "We shall have to send them a present, Julian and I. After all, it is only through their foolish snobbery that Julian and I found each other. Let me see, what shall we send them — perhaps a well-executed miniature of Hillcrest in all its glory? That should serve to put a bend or two in their branch, shouldn't it?"

"Lucy," Jennie interrupted, wishing to tell her the rest of her news as soon as possible, unwelcome as that news must be. "We didn't tell Lord Thorpe, although he must be informed shortly — we'll let Kit handle it — but we've had more news from London. It seems scandal wasn't enough — now the tongues are wagging about his lordship's possible involvement in the *way* Miss Anscom died. According to Amanda Delaney — who is quite incensed, let me tell you — some people are acting as if your Julian has already been found guilty of the crime. Much as it confounds Kit to say so, he believes your ideas about the letters to the papers were correct all along. Someone is out to see Lord Thorpe hanged."

"I knew it!" Lucy exploded, pounding her fists into the mattress on either side of her. "It may have taken a bit longer than I thought — although I remember Julian telling me how it is folly to overestimate the intelligence of the average peer — but it would seem Julian's enemy was not too farfetched in his plans. Thank goodness we shall soon be unmasking the man."

"You shall?" Jennie urged, already feeling better. "I thought something was up when Lord Thorpe asked Kit and Tristan to come to his library with him." A small frown appeared on her pretty face as she added, "Dexter wasn't invited along, though. Surely you don't mean —"

Lucy, exhaled in a frustrated sigh. "I don't know, Jennie. I've been lying here trying to put a face to the man who tried to murder me, but I just can't do it. I . . . I thought at the time that it was Julian."

"Dexter looks much like Julian, although he's a much smaller man," Jennie pointed out. "But I met Dexter last year when Kit and I were in town. He was such a likeable nodcock — I can scarcely believe him capable of such a heinous act."

Lucy pushed back the covers and got to her feet, walking to the window to look out over the grounds. "I certainly don't want to believe it either. But Dexter isn't the only suspect. Julian's secretary, his cousin Parker, is also very like Julian in his coloring — although his sallow complexion does not compliment his hair, and his taste in clothing rather runs to the drab and uninspiring. Then there's his expression — Aunt Rachel says it is rather like he had just swallowed a prune whole."

"Well, then?" Jennie urged. "Parker is our man. I trust your instincts, and if you don't like him, he's bound to be the one."

"I said I didn't like the cut of his clothes, Jennie. It doesn't necessarily follow that the man's a murderer. Besides, he was kidnapped not two nights ago, only to return here badly beaten. Much as I would like to think that Dexter is innocent, I can't imagine Parker being able to administer his own beating. No — it has to be someone we've overlooked. Somewhere there must be someone with either an ax to grind or a fortune to be made."

Jennie cudgeled her brain, trying to come up with a likely suspect. "Lord Seabrook!" she offered after some minutes. "He's got Lady Cynthia, after all."

Lucy snorted, wrinkling her pert nose. "She's no prize. Besides, Lord Seabrook would have wed a fat crone with warts if her fortune were big enough, and heaven knows we've got enough of that sort littering the ground all over London."

"Lucy, you're incorrigible!" Jennie scolded, highly amused.

Her cousin grinned unrepentantly and held up a finger, pointing out, "Ah, but am I right? Indeed I am." Her face fell slightly as she said wearily, "Which brings us back to our starting point, doesn't it? Pity — I would rather it had been Lord Seabrook myself."

Jennie, who had been sitting with her chin cupped in one palm, mused almost to herself, "You know, if I didn't know you better, I'd say you were the one who had the most to gain through all this."

"*What!*" Lucy squeaked incredulously, rounding on her cousin, her mouth agape. "*Me?*"

Nodding her head absently, Jennie ticked off her reasons on her fingertips. "One: you wanted Julian for yourself. After years of chasing him, your love turned to hate and you sought revenge. Two: you set up the entire scandal, although believing that you had taken an active hand in the seduction and murder of Miss Anscom leaves open the thought that you would have had to employ an accomplice. You made sure you were the one to rescue Thorpe the night of the Selbridge ball and then talked him into bringing you to Hillcrest. Three: once here, you insinuated yourself into his heart, causing him to propose marriage. Then, once Julian was convicted and executed, you would inherit the fortune he would be sure to leave you, along with the dower house and all the jewels that aren't entailed. My goodness — you would even inherit Dexter, in a manner of speaking."

"Dexter!" Lucy interrupted, listening in spite of herself. "Whatever would I do with Dexter?"

This puzzled Lady Bourne for a moment, but did not defeat her. "Dexter must be your accomplice. You both had so much to gain."

"You know," Lucy pointed out, giving her cousin a hug, "it's a good thing you compromised Kit into marrying you. You need a keeper."

"Well, it did make sense." Jennie

blushed, ashamed of herself for getting, as she was so prone to do, a bit carried away. "I'm sorry, pet."

"It certainly did make sense." Lucy agreed kindly. "Right up to the point where I drugged myself. Or was that just the enterprising Dexter double-crossing his accomplice?"

Jennie colored and shifted a bit in her chair. "I already said I was sorry, Lucy. Don't keep at me. Besides," she added, tipping her blond head to one side thoughtfully, "it isn't as if you and Dexter couldn't have had a falling-out —"

"Oh, give over, do," Lucy pleaded, dissolving into giggles at the thought of Dexter ever being able to take the place of Julian in her heart. "You just keep to loving your Kit and raising more beautiful babies like Christopher. I don't think you have it in you to be a very successful Bow Street Runner. Besides, I thought we had already ruled out Dexter as a likely suspect?"

"Did you?" came Rachel's voice from the doorway. "I don't know how you came to that conclusion, although I must say I agree with you. He just doesn't strike me as a murderer. Only one thing bothers me — he refuses to tell me where he spent

248

the winter; says he would be breaching a confidence or some such farrididdle. He could have secreted himself in this area, and that's how he struck up an acquaintance with the late Miss Anscom."

The two younger women turned to give Rachel their full attention. Their aunt was a highly intelligent and intuitive woman — as they both learned to their dismay the day they had hidden themselves in Lucy's father's study to read one of the books he kept on the topmost shelf. If Rachel had a theory, they were anxious to hear it.

"I pointed out to Dexter that his evasive attitude didn't exactly enhance his declarations of innocence, but he merely countered with the fact — one we seem to have disregarded — that Parker was with Julian for the whole of the time he resided at Hillcrest last winter. Having already in my mind dismissed Lady Cynthia, Lord Seabrook, and even Lucy here as being the guilty party, I would have to say that either Parker or Dexter is our man. I have just left Julian, my dear," she finished, looking at Lucy, "and it would seem he and the rest have come to much the same conclusion."

"You thought *I* could be guilty?" Lucy exclaimed, astonished, while Jennie looked at her smugly, as if to say, "I told you so."

Rachel patted her niece's hand. "I was just employing deductive reasoning, dearest. Of course I did not *really* consider you. Although I have to tell you that, if pushed, a court could make a mighty case against you. Why, Jennie, I thought you had left those monkey faces of yours in the nursery. Any moment now you will be sticking out your tongue. For shame."

"Yes, Aunt Rachel," Jennie agreed humbly, although her green eyes sparkled with mischief as she dodged Lucy's jabbing elbow.

"Well, we shall know soon enough," Lucy told them confidently, going over to the table beside her bed, picking up the button she had seen there earlier, and holding it up. "Thank goodness I had the good sense to hold on to this when my horse shied."

"Held on to it?" Rachel sniffed. "We had the devil's own time prying it away from you, the doctor and I. Where did you find it?"

"At the scene of the crime," she said, her voice lowering a full octave. "Find the owner of this button, ladies, and we shall have discovered our murderer. Which," she said, brightening, "is what I shall try to do tonight when we all gather for dinner."

There then ensued a heated argument, with Rachel and Jennie protesting that Lucy was still too weak to go downstairs and Lucy pooh-poohing their concern, saying her place was at Julian's side — and failing to mention that she felt the need to see him as soon as possible so that she could apologize for ever doubting him.

Julian was standing with his back to the doorway as Lucy, who had cajoled and co-erced Deirdre into helping her into her best gown before Aunt Rachel could show up and gainsay her, walked into the draw-ing room a full half-hour early for dinner.

Look at him, she told herself, standing there appearing to be so solemn as he gazes out over his land. Her heart showing a tendency to skip several beats, she lost no time in crossing the room to lay her head against his sleeve. "Julian, please, can you ever forgive me?" she asked, looking up into his face.

"Lucy! What are you doing out of bed?" Thorpe exclaimed, turning to clasp her bare upper arms. "I have already told ev-eryone you were still unconscious. Why did Rachel allow you to dress for dinner?"

"And hello to you too, dearest." Lucy

grinned, knowing that concern, not anger, colored his questions. "I'm here for several reasons, actually, the most important being that I can remember my atrocious behavior of last night and want nothing more than to throw myself at your feet and beg forgiveness for my stupidity. You must know I would never have thought to accuse you if I had been in control of my senses. I don't know how I could have been so silly."

"The Gypsy," Thorpe reminded her, sliding his hands down her arms to capture her fingers in his tight grip. "You know, darling, I do believe that old charlatan may have helped to save your life. I might not have been so suspicious otherwise when I saw you. Oh, Lucy," he breathed, drawing her against his chest. "You were such a sight, all bruised and turned in on yourself. I was never so frightened in my life. Promise me you'll never do anything like that again."

Lucy closed her eyes as she rubbed her face against his waistcoat. "I promise never to let anyone drug me ever again," she told him solemnly, then raised her face to grin at him. "Besides needlessly upsetting you, my dearest, the stuff tasted quite vile, you know. Although, if my memory serves me correctly, I do believe last night held a few pleasant moments, hmm?"

Julian lowered his head until his forehead touched hers. "You remember?" he asked huskily. "It was unforgiveable of me, taking advantage of you when you were powerless to fend me off."

"Yes," she agreed, wrapping her arms around his waist beneath his jacket. "Your behavior was utterly reprehensible. Julian," she asked, dimpling, "do you promise to be reprehensible again just as soon as you are able? Perhaps later this evening, when I am more awake? My memories are quite pleasant, but regrettably vague."

"You cheeky wench!" Julian said, delighted all over again by her unabashed openness when it came to expressing her feelings. "However did I exist without you?"

"I can't imagine," she answered airily, pulling his mouth down to within an inch of hers. "But I do believe I can now foretell your fortune, if you'd care to be enlightened. Ah, my blond god of happiness, your days will be filled with love and laughter forevermore, and your nights, ah, yes, those lovely nights, will be spent like this."

Their lips came together in a long kiss that swiftly brought back the powerful feelings that had sprung up between them in the dark hours of the early morning. As they strained together, heedless of their surroundings, all thoughts of murderers and deceitful plots flew out of their minds, and for those too-brief moments in time they were as lovers have always been, totally enmeshed in each other.

But they were not to be left alone for long, as the sound of approaching footsteps brought Thorpe, cursing under his breath, back to his senses. "Stand here beside me," he told Lucy seriously as he turned them toward the open doorway.

"Hmmm," Lucy agreed happily, smiling inanely as Rachel entered the room ready to scold her errant charge. But one look at Lucy's dreamy expression, and Rachel, who had not spent her entire life squiring her niece about, could only sigh resignedly and shake her head. Clearly her days as chaperon were coming to an end. Thank goodness. Tristan didn't require her services — it was more than time she set up an establishment of her own. Besides, she thought, smiling inwardly, Tristan and I would kill each other within a sennight if we were forced to deal with each other too closely.

Julian had just had time to pour each of

the ladies glasses of sherry before the rest of their party arrived — Jennie looking delightfully radiant as she walked in beside Kit, and Dexter looking very out of place in his role of supporting prop to his still-swollen-faced cousin Parker. Tristan was the last to arrive, and he merely nodded at Thorpe before positioning himself near the doorway, his shoulder propped against the wall.

The actors were all in place, Julian observed, lifting his glass to his lips as his cold gray eyes surveyed the room and its occupants. It was time for the play to begin.

"You're looking fighting fit," Dexter told Lucy as he sat down after helping Parker into a chair. "According to Julian, you were at death's door, but I see he has exaggerated the thing out of all proportion. Julian, dear fellow," he said, looking up at his cousin, "you're like an old hen with one chick. When I told poor Parker here what you said about Lucy's condition, the man nearly expired with shock. I'd be careful if I were you — it just might be you have a rival vying for Lucy's affections."

Leave it to Dexter to get straight to the heart of things, Julian thought sardonically, even if he doesn't have the slightest idea of the importance of what he has just said. Exchanging a knowing look with Tristan, who had straightened his posture at Dexter's words, Thorpe walked over to stand in front of Parker. "So you were worried about Lucy, were you, cousin?"

Parker touched a shaking hand to his discolored eye. "Yes . . . yes, of course," he agreed shakily. "I'm aware of your high regard for Miss Gladwin, and the thought of anything happening to cause you any more pain was very distressing to me."

"Yes." The earl smiled his agreement. "I must remember how very loyal you are to me, Parker. Lucy would be wise to look to you for comfort if I am to soon be clapped into jail for the murder of Miss Anscom. As my countess, which she will be before the week is out, she must needs lean heavily on your knowledge of my affairs."

"Then you do intend to marry her?"

"Ah, cousin," Julian gibed, shaking his head, "surely you have already figured that out for yourself. Isn't that why you went to her room last night and poured laudanum down her throat — so that you wouldn't have rid yourself of me just to be left with an inconvenient countess to share the wealth?"

"What?" Dexter, the only member of the party who had not been privy to any of the events of the previous evening, leapt to his feet, his eyes on Lucy. "You were drugged? By *Parker?* Why in blue blazes hasn't anyone told me?"

Lucy shrugged apologetically. "Because you were our other suspect, Dex, I'm sorry to say. But do wait awhile before flying up into the boughs, for I want to hear the rest of what Julian has to say. There is more, isn't there?" she asked her fiancé.

Parker huddled in his chair, speechless, as Julian expanded on his theme. "There certainly is more, quite a bit more, but we shall require Parker's assistance in order to fill in a few gaps. To begin with the beginning, I suggest we go back to this past winter, and my residence at Hillcrest. It was during this time that you first met Susan Anscom, wasn't it, Parker?"

"I don't know what you're talking about!" the secretary denied hotly. "I never even met Sue Anscom!"

"*Sue?*" Rachel put in pointedly. "Methinks he dost protest too much, don't you?"

"Aunt Rachel, *sshh,*" Jennie whispered, quite caught up in things.

"You met Susan Anscom, seduced her,

then talked her into going along with your dirty little scheme," Thorpe persisted, his voice still deadly calm. "Tell me, was murdering Miss Anscom always a part of your plot, or were you initially only out to destroy my good name?"

Parker looked around the room, knowing himself to be the center of attention, and his formerly fearful expression faded, to be replaced by a smile of utmost satisfaction. After years of blending in with the woodwork, being overlooked, dismissed, and discounted, he was suddenly the most important person amid a roomful of some of England's most respected peers. "It was my idea from start to finish." He sneered, sitting up proudly. "Sue thought I was helping her into compromising you into marriage, but I only told her that to keep her in line. I wrote the suicide notes, copying her handwriting from her journal. Stupid cow — as if I was going to all that trouble so that she could end up a countess."

"And then you killed her," Lucy put in, fascinated in spite of herself. "Tell me, Parker, was it your child she carried?"

He threw back his head and laughed aloud. "Child?" he mocked. "There was no child. That was a last-minute inspiration of mine — rather like the finishing icing atop a cake. Her seduction alone wasn't enough, just like disgracing Julian was no longer enough. I always believed I would be a much better earl than he — society might turn a blind eye to Sue's suicide, but it wouldn't overlook a man who had murdered his own unborn child." His smile faded and then he looked down at the hands he had clasped tightly in his lap. "But it took too long for those fools to act — couldn't they see Sue had been murdered?" He glared at Julian. "You should have been arrested by now. And then *she* began to meddle," he complained, jerking his head in Lucy's direction. "I had to be rid of her."

"Naughty puss," Kit Wilde observed mildly. "I always said you were a bit too much of an independent thinker. Jennie would have been content to let me do the sleuthing. I can see why friend Parker here was so put out with you."

Lucy bristled, but then remembered the button she had found and smiled ruefully. "I begin to see Parker's point, much as it pains me. If we were to inspect his jackets, I believe we might just find the one to which this button belongs." She held up the bone button so that all could see. "I stumbled upon it beside the pool. Miss Anscom must not have agreed with all of Parker's plans and put up a bit of a struggle. You know," she said thoughtfully, "I'm rather distressed that Julian has beat me to it, but I still don't totally understand how he figured it out. Julian?"

"Not yet," Dexter contradicted, clearly quite angry. "I want to hear why he thought I was a suspect, drat it all anyway. I'm highly insulted, coz, and I don't mind saying so."

Julian bowed deeply in his cousin's direction, as Tristan slipped silently behind Parker. "My deepest apologies, Dex. But as my heir, you had to be a suspect."

"And that's another thing," Dexter said, scratching his head. "I *am* the heir. Even if Parker had succeeded in having you hanged, he wouldn't have inherited the title. I stood in his way."

Lord Rule's deep voice made Parker jump slightly in his chair. "Somehow I don't believe that trifling incidental would have deterred our man Parker for very long."

"Why, you . . ." Dexter swore, lunging toward the secretary, only to halt in his tracks as Parker jumped to his feet, a small silver pistol in his hand.

"Stay away from me, all of you," he warned, moving the pistol about nervously.

"Give it up, Parker," Julian advised smoothly, holding out his hand to show him the bullets Bartholomew had discovered in his room. "And on the off chance you had more of these things hidden elsewhere, I also took the liberty of removing the firing pin. You have often remarked on your dislike of firearms of any sort, and it occurred to me that you would have a pistol only if you felt in need of protection. A guilty man would feel that way, wouldn't he?"

Parker seemed to crumble where he stood. "All for nothing," he mumbled self-pityingly. "All for nothing."

"Yes," Julian agreed, removing the pistol from Parker's slack grip. "I only wish you hadn't gone to the trouble of hiring some local to rearrange your face in order to prove your loyalty. Lord Rule ran the man to earth this afternoon in the village, so there's no sense denying it. Yes, it's a pity. It would have afforded me the greatest pleasure to have smashed you into a pulp."

"I'll take him to the constable," Tristan offered, grabbing Parker none too gently by the elbow and leading the man away. "Kit," he asked, "care to ride along? If we're lucky, the worm will try to make a break for it."

"Trifling incidental?" Dexter repeated dully, looking at Rachel for comfort. "Am I really a trifling incidental?"

"Of course you're not," Rachel soothed, slipping an arm about the young dandy's slim shoulders. "Jennie, let us adjourn to the morning room, where we can ask Raleigh to bring Dexter here a bracing cup of tea, as dinner will certainly be late. Poor Dexter," she clucked as the two ladies led the disillusioned young man from the room.

"It's over," Julian breathed, once he and Lucy were alone in the room. "At long last it's over."

Lucy shook her head, hiding her eyes from him. "Not quite, Julian. I would not be fair if I did not point out that you are now free to marry Lady Cynthia. She's engaged to Lord Seabrook now, but I can't believe she wouldn't take you back once she learns your name has been cleared of scandal."

Julian assumed a thoughtful expression. "I see," he said consideringly. "But what about you, Lucy? I have compromised you a half-dozen times at least. Wouldn't you object?"

Lucy looked up at him with much the lively expression she had shown when successfully handling her hobbyhorse in the park. "Object, Julian? Goodness no. Not me. Why, I should simply resume my pursuit of you with renewed fervor until I had won you back again. What do you think of my secreting myself in your bedchamber and draping my scantily clad body across the bottom of your bed?"

Sweeping her up high into his arms, Julian threw back his head as Lucy dropped butterfly kisses all over his face. "Sounds promising, pet," he growled deep in his throat. "Tell me more."

EPILOGUE

"Oh, poor Dexter," Lucy wailed, bringing her hobbyhorse to a halt beside the stylishly clad young exquisite who was just then sprawling inelegantly on the grass in the middle of the park, his fallen hobbyhorse at his side. "I told you not to try that hill until you had a bit more experience."

"Drat it all, Lucy, I was doing just fine till that show-off husband of yours cut me off. Whose idea was this expedition anyway?"

Julian, having already dismounted from his vehicle, strolled over to give Dexter a hand in getting to his feet. "After more than a year of marriage to Lucy, I'm afraid I have been totally corrupted. Forgive me, Dex, but this excursion was my idea."

"You don't do things by half-measures, do you, coz?" Dexter gibed, brushing himself down and then sighing over the grass stain on his left knee. "And to think you used to look down your nose at my exploits. There are times, Julian, when you make me feel like a very old man. Why don't you be a good fellow and go set up your nursery awhile — it may mature you, settle you down a tad."

Winking broadly at his wife, who just as broadly winked back at him, Thorpe refrained from comment. There was time and enough for children next year, he and Lucy had decided. For now they were content to explore all the joys in life that he had previously overlooked — and his Lucy made an excellent teacher.

"Have a slight accident?" asked Lord Rule, who had ridden up atop his pitch-black stallion. "Have a care, Rutherford, else you'll break that leg again."

"How did you know — ?" Dexter was startled into saying before he stopped and amended, "Me? I never heard such foolishness. I never broke anything in my life — except a few bottles after dinner, of course."

"That's not what I heard from the lady," Tristan quipped, raising one dark brow. "Nursed you all winter a year ago right here in her rooms above the milliner's shop over past Piccadilly."

"So that's where you were!" Lucy leered, giving Dexter a playful poke in the ribs. "Does this lady have a name?"

"I slipped on the stairs as I was leaving

late one night," Dexter explained into his cravat. "Julian," he then pleaded, raising his head, "call her off, please!"

"*Hmm?*" Julian questioned blankly, for his mind had been on other things. He had tried not to think overmuch about the events of the previous year, but Tristan's mentioning of the subject, even vaguely, had recalled it all to his mind. He repressed a slight shudder as he remembered the last time he had visited his cousin in Ringmoor, the well-run asylum he had placed Parker in after the man had broken down completely on the way to jail. "Oh, look," he improvised, trying to change the subject. "There's Sir Henry and his ward, Mary. Pet, didn't you say Rachel was presenting her for Sir Henry?"

"Yes, indeed," Lucy agreed, happy to see that the slight cloud that had passed across her husband's features was now gone. "Aunt Rachel's doing it as a special favor to Sir Henry. Isn't Miss Lawrence a pretty thing?" she added, looking at the young lady in question as the open carriage moved off down a side path. "Aunt Rachel must still be writing that book of hers, and declined to ride along. Isn't it famous that we have a budding Jane Austen in our midst!"

Tristan's dark eyes were following the progress of the carriage, his expression thoughtful. "What?" he asked, scarcely believing what he had heard. "Rachel is penning a novel? My God, I sincerely hope she isn't using any of us in her book."

Lucy cocked her head to one side and considered her cousin as he sat so proudly in the saddle. "Oh, I don't know, Tristan. I think you would make a marvelous hero — tall, dark, handsome, and oh so mysterious."

"What about me?" Dexter pouted. "Wouldn't I make a good hero? Rachel has my permission to use me in her book."

Julian draped a companionable arm around his cousin's shoulder. "If she has a part in there for a village idiot, I'll be sure to suggest your name, coz," he teased affectionately, causing Lucy and Tristan to break into laughter.

"Look at them," Lady Seabrook sniffed, pointing one kid-encased finger at the small but noisy party of people standing on the grass. "They're making spectacles of themselves as usual. I should never think to so demean myself."

Lord Seabrook, who had been eyeing the group with something akin to envy, replied flatly, "Yes, my dear, I know."

Lady Seabrook was about to ask her husband just exactly what he meant by his statement when Julian, uncaring of any audience, leaned down to place a firm kiss smack on his wife's lips. "Well!" Lady Seabrook exclaimed, drawing herself up stiffly. "I never!"

Lord Seabrook flicked the reins and urged his matched pair into movement, never taking his eyes off the clearly happy couple. "No, Cynthia," he sighed with the resigned air of a man who knew what he had as well as what he had missed, "that much is true. You never — never have, and never will. Pity . . ."

As Dexter remounted his hobbyhorse, he chanced to see Lord and Lady Seabrook as they passed in the promenade. "Hoo! If it isn't Lord and Lady Seaweed. They don't seem to be enjoying themselves, do they? I hear he sold off half his stable at Tatt's last week. Do you think he's retrenching?"

"Gambling," Tristan supplied knowingly, for there was little that went on in London that Tristan did not know of one way or another, although Lucy found it impossible to learn much of anything about his life, no matter how she prodded. Tipping his hat, Tristan then bid them all a fine day and turned his horse in the direction Sir Henry's carriage had taken, although Lucy and the others were not to know that. Mary Lawrence was an enigma; he couldn't seem to get a handle on her and her relationship to Sir Henry. And Tristan didn't like loose ends.

As they watched Rule ride off, Lucy tapped her fingernail against her teeth as she leaned back into Julian's embrace. "If only Tristan would settle down, get married. He seems so restless."

"Here now," Julian protested. "Kit tells me Jennie believes herself in charge of settling everyone she knows into comfortable little niches. Don't tell me you are about to go poaching on her private territory?"

"Jennie's efforts have met with precious little success so far, love," Lucy pointed out, now gnawing on her knuckle as she tilted her head and thought some more. "Perhaps it is time I exerted myself a bit on Tristan's behalf. A man isn't truly happy, truly fulfilled, until he is married."

"Perhaps Tristan is the exception, pet?" Julian suggested, resting his chin on her hair.

"No," she denied such ridiculousness out of hand. "It's simply that he hasn't yet found the right woman." Just then an idea struck her and she whirled about abruptly to throw her arms around her husband's neck. "Oh, you most wonderful, intelligent man!" she exclaimed, giving him a smacking kiss on the cheek. "The exception! That's who we shall find for Tristan — the Exception to the Rule!"

Dexter slipped away quietly, his sympathies with Tristan, but inwardly thankful that no one considered his flightly self to be good husband material. Married — him? "Then I'd really be the village idiot!" he muttered under his breath, and pushed off down the hill.

Lord and Lady Thorpe, just then gazing contentedly into each other's eyes, never even noticed that he was gone.

We hope you have enjoyed this Large Print book. Other Thorndike, Wheeler or Chivers Press Large Print books are available at your library or directly from the publishers.

For more information about current and upcoming titles, please call or write, without obligation, to:

Publisher
Thorndike Press
295 Kennedy Memorial Drive
Waterville, ME   04901
Tel. (800) 223-1244

Or visit our Web site at:
www.gale.com/thorndike
www.gale.com/wheeler

OR

Chivers Large Print
published by BBC Audiobooks Ltd
St James House, The Square
Lower Bristol Road
Bath BA2 3SB
England
Tel. +44(0) 800 136919
email: bbcaudiobooks@bbc.co.uk
www.bbcaudiobooks.co.uk

All our Large Print titles are designed for easy reading, and all our books are made to last.